ADEPT'S PATH

A TEER & KARD STORY

Faolan's Pen Publishing
22 King St. S, Suite 300
Waterloo, Ontario
N2J 1N8 Canada

A record of this book is available from Library and Archives Canada.

Printed in the United States of America
1 2 3 4 5 6 7 8 9 10
First edition
ISBN 978-1-989674-91-8 (Trade Paperback)
ISBN 978-1-989674-92-5 (Amazon Paperback)

ADEPT'S PATH

A TEER & KARD STORY

GLYNN STEWART

FAOLAN'S PEN
PUBLISHING

faolanspen.com

1

It said everything about the strange state of Teer's mind that the thick mountain snow was both comfortingly familiar and exotically strange. In Teer's barely nineteen turnings on the world, he'd seen deep snow as an occasional thing on the windswept plains of the central prairie. Snow was common near his stepfather's ranch, but more of a dusting that colored the grass in white and was swiftly carried away by the wind.

But sixty turnings of another man's memories lived in Teer's head. Abray had spent almost half of his life in the Latch Mountains, a range of rounded-but-still-towering peaks that crossed the eastern side of old Zeeanan territory.

This far south, snow covered the peaks all through the turning, and the upper slopes saw deep snow through half of it. Abray had been intimately familiar with the snows and features of his chosen exile, and if the area was no longer part of the Unity's frontier, it didn't look like anyone had been down this particular valley in months.

Teer's mare, Star, stepped carefully through the snow. She was even less familiar with the deep covering than her rider, since she didn't have any of Abray's memories and had been kept home when heavy snows swept the ranch.

"At least anyone hunting us is going to have as much difficulty with the snow as us," Teer's companion said.

A spark of anger ran through Teer, one that he managed to suppress with the skill of tendays of practice now. Teer had thought *he* was angry at the Spehari who ruled the Unity—he'd been angry enough to try to shoot one once, which had turned out to be his current companion Kard.

Abray's fury made Teer's anger look like a childish tantrum. The memories in his head were of the last Adept of the Merik Orders, a warrior-monk sworn to the service of the Unity. Except that the Spehari had decided that the Merik Adepts, magic-users who were immune to Spehari mental domination, were too great a risk.

Teer now had the memories of the dark day that Spehari Captain-Magistrates had led Merik musketeers into the monastery Abray had lived in. Of the formal greeting party led by confused Masters, including Abray, that had turned to bloodshed.

Abray's memories weren't clear on how he'd survived. He suspected he'd been knocked unconscious and left for dead, becoming the sole survivor of a monastery of over three hundred Adepts.

Those memories were now Teer's. The anger that came with them *wasn't* Teer's, but it was hard to control. He knew that Kard was *not* Spehari, that the half-blood El-Spehari had been just as used and betrayed as the Merik Adepts had once been, but the dual angers that burned within him struggled to separate his companion from the species.

"A pursuit will ride in our trail," Teer said, his tone as calm as he could manage. That realization was exactly what Kard wanted him to have, of course. Even as Teer struggled with the new memories in his head, his friend and companion—legally his master, with a magical bond between them that made Teer Kard's property by Unity law— continued to try to teach him.

"We will need to dismount before we go much farther," he continued. "If the memories are true, the path ahead is uneven. The snow will pack enough to protect the horses from their own weight but not ours."

That knowledge was *Teer's*, not Abray's. Abray knew the terrain of this valley, but he'd never known horses well, even before he'd spent most of his life hiding in the mountains.

"Good thought," Kard agreed. He swung down from Clack, his gray gelding, and sank into the snow up to the top of his riding boots with a disgruntled squelch.

Kard wore the same heavy gray duster as Teer. It was the "uniform" outfit of a licensed Unity bounty hunter, a thick multi-layered jacket with armor plates sewn into it. It would be proof against the cold of the mountain, though Kard's hung open and Teer had buttoned his up.

The snow was cold around Teer's ankles as he dismounted as well. Six inches deep, he judged, and he felt bad for subjecting the horses to it. It wasn't like they could clear the snow away ahead of the animals, not without using Kard's magic and drawing even more attention.

The El-Spehari, after all, were proscribed by the Unity now. Outside of a handful sworn directly to the King in Winter, they weren't supposed to exist. If discovered, Kard would be executed—and he'd revealed himself to *save* one of that handful of "loyal" El-Spehari during the mess that had given Teer another man's memories.

They had more problems than they could count these days—and going as far west into civilization as they had wasn't the best way to avoid the Unity's Inquisition.

But this valley was where Teer's memory said Abray had lived, and Teer needed to see it. To begin to understand the man who now only existed in his mind.

———

ABRAY'S MEMORIES seemed to grow clearer with each passing step. He'd known this piece of mountain like the back of his hand, and while the trees had changed, the landscape remained almost identical.

Teer let those old memories guide him. He wasn't even certain *how* old those memories were—when Abray had died, this region of the Latch Mountains had been home to a small village that had existed almost entirely to support the sole inn in the pass through the range, and that settlement was now a large town by the maps they'd purchased on their way there.

Still, there was no question in his mind as to his route and destination. The valley they were following was a dip in the mountain, carved by spring snowmelt over the centuries, and several offshoots split off from it as they went higher. Few of them looked large enough for people, let alone horses, and he was surprised to realize the one he was looking for was more visible now than in Abray's memories.

He paused and took his bearings, as it looked like part of the mountain had slid away, opening the path further and clearing away the trees that had shielded the path from passing eyes—not that there would have *been* any eyes up there.

"Teer?" Kard asked.

"It's that way," he replied, gesturing. "There was a rockslide since Abray left, so it didn't look quite right, and I needed to check the other landmarks. Least the mountains are the same!"

Kard stepped up next to him, his paler skin blending better with the snow around them than Teer's dark Merik coloring. Even a pure Spehari was far darker than snow, but Teer looked more like shadowed tree bark than anything else.

"This guiding ourselves by a dead man's memory is strange, even to me," the El-Spehari said in a slow drawl, surveying the mountains. "And the back of my neck is itching. I keep expecting my father's people to emerge from the trees—or for Storm to come back."

Storm—more properly *the scent of air after the storm*, the thought-concept used by a telepathic brain-eating lizard larger than a man to define himself—had been the callipsus patriarch who'd led the attack on Shellsvan and who had plunged Abray's memories into Teer's head to distract him at a critical moment.

It had worked and Storm had nearly killed Teer—but Abray's memories included the Adept's training in healing trances, and Teer had every magical gift required to be an Adept.

He just had no idea what he was *doing* with those gifts. Drawing on Abray's memories, that was changing, but even with the full knowledge of the last Adept in his head, it was taking time for him to turn those memories into useful skills.

"I need… what goes 'round these memories," Teer said slowly, stretching for words he didn't have.

"Context," Kard suggested. He'd been trained by the best schools and teachers the Unity possessed, the half-blood children of the Spehari a valued tool to their parents and one worth the investment.

Teer had been taught by his mother in a farmhouse. He was literate and could handle the books for a large ranch, but complex language was beyond him.

"*Context*," he repeated the word. "I guess? Abray was a strange man, I think, even when he was with the Orders. But he was in these mountains for longer than I've been alive, Kard. Something here… might help me understand."

"We can't go much farther west. You might be able to," his friend allowed, "but I can't."

"I know."

There was a sharp dogleg in the cleft. Teer recognized it—and saw the spot where the dogleg had created a smoother rise out of the gouge. Water would spill over the edge there and run down the mountain into a different channel, rendering this path unusable in spring, but at this time of the turning, it was the easiest access into Abray's homestead.

He led Star up the gentle slope and turned. To the left of the broad meltwater channel, pristine snow led into a sheltered dell. Trees rose out of it, some taller and some shorter than in the memories, but even the needles of the evergreens showed the lack of wind in the sheltered hollow.

Instinct took over then, guiding his feet along a path that no one had tread in turnings upon turnings. He stepped between the trees, letting the memories take him toward the central clearing he figured was still there—it might have shrunk without Abray's axe clearing it for firewood, but the stone outcropping that had created the gap wouldn't have gone away.

Teer emerged from the trees into that gap and stopped.

If Abray's memories were right, his house had been right *there*, a multi-roomed structure of hand-shaped logs that had been built onto the outcropping. Even after fifty or even a hundred turnings, Teer would have expected to see ruins of some kind.

Instead, only the open space amidst the trees and a vague rise in the snow marked where the stone outcropping might be, and Teer was suddenly very, very lost.

2

Teer just stood there for a moment. It took solid focus not to slide into Abray at the missing house, keeping his sense of who *he* was solid and center in his thoughts.

It was rare for him to become Abray now, though there had been a few rough moments in the beginning. To stand in front of what had been the man's home and see *nothing* was hard, and all the harder for how much he'd been using the memories to get there.

"Teer." Kard's voice was level behind him. With the link between them, the El-Spehari had a solid sense of what Teer was feeling and thinking at any given moment.

Teer's sense of *Kard's* feelings and thoughts was stronger. The bond was intended to make it easier for Teer to serve as the other man's servant, after all, even if Kard had only created it with Teer's permission and to save the younger man's life.

"The house should be here."

Teer took a solid breath and stepped forward. Star paced after him, the horse unbothered. She was certain the two-legged half of the party knew what was going on.

If only he could be so sure of himself as his horse was!

He walked forward to where his memories said the front door should have been.

"There should be a stone outcrop under the snow," he said aloud. "I —I mean, *Abray*—built a cabin, using it as a wall to start. Later, he managed to get his hands on the right tools and leveled the stone out to use as a foundation. He carved the stone he took down into slabs he used to extend the foundation over time, anchoring the wood he took from the trees.

"He started with an axe, and he built an entire little farm. A home, for him and Opal."

Opal was the woman Abray had saved from wolfen venom in the forests of the lower slopes. The rest of her caravan had died to the dangerous creatures, but Abray had arrived in time to save her from them—and his knowledge of local herbs and his Adept magic had saved her life.

She'd lived in the little trading post for five turnings after that, before the day she'd come to visit Abray and never left. It had been clearly planned on her part, but Abray hadn't seen it coming.

Somehow, Teer suspected the sixty turnings of the other man's memories weren't going to be much use with his romantic shortcomings. His only saving grace there, so far as he knew, was that he was pretty.

"It was a lot of work, even for an Adept with his skills," Teer continued aloud. "Except now I don't know if it happened, because I can't see any sign of it."

It was bad enough having the memories of a dead man in his head —including the memory of Storm *eating* Abray at the end of his life— but if those memories were wrong or fabricated by Storm, he had no idea what traps might be laid in them.

Kard took Star's reins from him silently, walking the horses over to the trees and tying them off to let Teer think.

Not that thinking was helping. He just stared at the pristine snow in front of him and focused on his breathing and the meditation exercises Abray had learned who-knew-how-long before.

It didn't escape his notice that he was using tools from Abray's memories to protect his sense of self *from* Abray's memories. The word *irony* was something else he'd taken from the other man's education.

Abray hadn't been as well educated as Kard, Teer didn't think, but he'd been far better educated than *Teer*.

"He built the whole place himself?" Kard asked. "Cut down trees, shaped them, carved stone, laid foundations?"

"Yeah. It took turnings and he only did... half of it, I think, before his wife joined him. He had to learn some of the skills on his own, even."

"He was an Adept, like you. Except he knew what he was doing." There was no accusation in the El-Spehari's voice, which Teer appreciated. He didn't know how long it had been since Abray died, but he *did* know how old Kard was—just past a hundred and twenty turnings.

That extra century came with surprisingly little talking down to Teer.

"I'm pulling exercises and tricks from his memories, but I have to be careful." The Merik man shrugged. "He *hated* your father's people. Though I don't think he knew anything about El-Spehari."

"Makes sense, since I didn't know anything about Adepts," Kard pointed out. "Which means that march on the monastery you remember was before my time. Even if he was here for thirty turnings, he died a *long* time ago, Teer.

"What would you expect to find here?"

"Some kind of sign." Teer wasn't sure. "Ruins? He built the house from solid logs and stone, after all."

There was a long silence, then Kard chuckled bitterly.

"You do know what that likely means, right?"

"No." Teer looked at his mentor crossly.

"To me, Teer, that sounds like it was intact enough that someone came across it and went, *Hey, look, free building material,*" Kard told him. "Because I would bet stones to blue shards that the beams and stones an Adept made for his home would be a lot better than those someone on the frontier could find.

"Someone probably pulled a wagon up here, some time in the last seventy turnings, and hauled away everything left of Abray's life. If you could somehow trace the work of his hands, I imagine those beams and blocks are now scattered through Cossax."

The image of a work crew dismantling Abray's carefully built home into pieces to build other houses brought a spike of white-hot rage to Teer... and also a moment of pride and compassion.

Better that the house serve than be lost entirely to the elements, he supposed.

"How would we..."

Teer trailed off halfway through the question as he saw the orange sparks of Kard's magic flare to life in front of him. Several square yards of snow were shifted away as if by a giant knife, lifting up to form a bank in what would have been Abray's living room.

The removed snow cleared the ground where the entrance had been—and Abray had put thought and effort into it when he'd built the final entrance. He'd carved the foundation of that part of the house directly from the native stone, and there was no mistaking the hand-smoothed surface of the steps or the chiseled anchor points for the walls.

Teer sighed in relief.

"I don't know what the house looked like," Kard said wryly, "but that sure looks like someone carved a foundation into that stone to me."

"Aye," Teer confirmed. "So, there is something here after all."

"This is your story we're following, Teer. What do we do now?"

Teer was quiet for a few moments. He wasn't sure. He hadn't had much of a plan, only the need to confirm that the house was here, that Abray had been *real*.

"I needed to know the man was real," he finally admitted. He snorted as a thought struck him, and he turned slowly. "And if this were the front, then the structure they weren't going to break down for parts would be... over there."

He stepped off into the woods. The trees there were no shorter than those around them, despite this having been the area Abray had cleared. At least seventy turnings, as Kard had pointed out. If the Adepts had been destroyed the same turning Kard entered the Unity's service, Abray would have died seventy-five turnings before.

It was a terrifying thought, but he buried it under a mix of amusement and recognition when he *did* find the ruin he was looking for. It had been a sturdy-enough shed when it was built, sturdy enough to survive the weather and time.

But however intact it had been when the rest of the house was dismantled, no one had seen any reason to take down Abray's outhouse.

Somehow, staring at the collapsed tiny building—a tree had grown *through* it at some point, which was part of what was keeping it as visible as it was!—and remembering it made everything seem that bit more real.

"Well, we've come a long way to find the place a dead man shit," Kard said. "I know you need this, Teer, but is there anything else? The farm you mentioned—it's gone. The trees took it back. The house is gone. We don't even know where his body is to bury."

Teer was moving as Kard's last few words hit home. He knew what he'd needed to come back to Abray's homestead for now.

Teer collected the folding shovel from Star's saddlebags, giving the mare a few gentle pets to assure her that he'd be back to brush her down shortly, then let Abray's memories guide him through the dell.

The spot he was looking for was still clear of trees. His memories led him directly to a small gap in the evergreens, marked by the skeletal winter remains of a pair of large redflower bushes.

Planting those two bushes had been the last thing Abray had done before leaving his home forever, and Teer shivered at the size of them now. Yet, despite untold turnings of growth, the bushes formed a natural horseshoe shape, defining the ground above Opal's grave.

He stood there looking at the clearing in silence for he didn't know how long, then set to work with the folding shovel. Clearing the snow from the grave wasn't a fast process, but it went smoothly enough.

The cairn of carefully arranged rock he uncovered was the reason why the bushes hadn't retaken the gravesite. Even in early winter, the snow had already smothered the groundcover that had moved into the stones, but the cairn was definitely the worse for wear.

Teer had expected that. He judged the plants with a cautious eye, assessing how much work he was going to need to do, then kept clearing.

The marker was where he'd expected it to be, toppled over at some point since Abray had chiseled Opal's name into it and set it in the ground. She was buried deep beneath the stones, beyond the reach of predators, but the stones had been intended to do what they had done: keep the stubborn plant life of a mountainside forest from growing over her grave.

Picking up the stone, Teer ran his fingers down over it, letting the memory of Abray's emotions pull him along. Then his fingers hit a crack in the stone and he shivered, moving the marker into place and examining it carefully.

Abray hadn't been a skilled-enough stonemason to recognize the flaw in the slab he'd hastily, if carefully, carved for Opal. Water had seeped into it and winter had done its harsh work. A third of the slab, including the first letter of Opal's name, had sheared clean away from the rest.

Teer had no idea how long ago the slab had broken in two, but he hadn't noticed the damage at first glance. Someone had put the pieces back together. Careful hands had laid in layers of mortar, even re-carving part of a damaged letter to match the original inscription.

The stone marker was probably heavy, but Teer didn't even notice as Abray's memories swept over him, along with a relief that wasn't truly his—but that he wouldn't reject.

He crouched back on his heels, running his fingers along the mortar line.

"Loua," he whispered aloud, the name coming to mind without focus. Loua and Marie, a Zeeanan and Merik woman respectively, had been the couple that had hosted Opal in Cossax, the nearby village, before she'd come to live with Abray.

Marie had been the blacksmith's sister and Loua had been the town's "artisan of all trades," and the closest thing they'd had to a stonemason. Loua would have been the only one able to repair a stone marker like this—and Loua and Marie had known where the homestead was.

Crouching next to Opal's grave, Abray's memories filled in the pieces for Teer. The two strong-willed and warm-hearted women had been the heart of Cossax at the time, and they'd come into the mountains to check on Opal every so often.

They'd have come up looking for Opal and found the house empty. They'd have found Opal's grave and paid their respects. Anything Abray had forgotten or done wrong in his hurry to close up the house would have been taken care of.

They'd probably have left a note, telling him to come visit them or else. Then they'd have come back every so often to check on the house, to see if Abray had returned.

Teer knew that Abray had quite possibly been dead before they'd even come up the first time. He'd definitely been dead by the second time they would have checked on the house. But the couple would have kept coming, making sure the house didn't deteriorate too badly and that Opal's grave was kept up.

And when Abray hadn't been back for a couple of turnings, they would have slowly started to "borrow" items from the homestead. It would have started with the metal tools, Teer figured. He'd grown up in a frontier community and he knew how hard those could be to source—or afford, even when they were available.

"Teer?" Kard said, putting his hand gently on Teer's shoulder and gripping. "This was his wife's grave, huh?"

"Yeah." Teer blinked away tears. "I think… friends of hers came up here lookin' for 'em. Fixed her marker when it broke, kept the bushes back long enough for 'em to be shaped forever.

"Took the house apart when they couldn't keep it up stopping by once a turning. He'd have been gone… ten, maybe even twenty, turnings by then, depending on how stubborn they were."

And Loua and Marie had been *very* stubborn.

"Somehow, knowing it wasn't all torn down by scavengers helps," he continued. "Abray would have *wanted* Loua and Marie to have his stuff, as much as he'd have wanted anyone to."

There was something in Abray's memories about Loua and Marie's daughters, but Teer found himself refusing to examine it. A feeling that perhaps some things were best left private, even when you had all of another man's memories.

Kard was quiet for a while, just standing there with his hand on Teer's shoulder.

"It's cold, but we should be able to get the weeds out of the cairn," he said. "Clean things up so it'll be clear for a few more turnings. I'm not thinking Abray's friends are likely to have been by in recent turnings."

Healthy and vibrant as Abray's memories of the couple were, they'd have been near Kard's age if they'd still lived… and only the most valued of the Spehari's servants had access to the food and care needed to live that long.

"Aye. No one has been here in a while. Let's… get it clean."

ONCE THEY'D CLEANED up the gravesite, the two men set up camp where the house would have been. Their gear was mostly intended for cold winds on the prairie, but Teer tested his bedroll, and it seemed to be waterproof enough for sleeping on top of the snow.

Abray's memories pointed out a few easy and small things he could add to the setup to make sure they'd be able to camp in snow. Teer could even see how they'd work from his own experience—he'd just never needed them before.

He might, he supposed. Most of his and Kard's activities in the turning since he'd entered the El-Spehari's service had been in the northern half of the eastern frontier. If they headed south, his understanding was that even the open regions started to see heavy snow in winter, but anyone looking for Kard would have to find an entirely new trail.

Kard had the fire going by the time Teer had brushed the horses down and checked on their feedbags. They easily swapped over the space by the blaze, allowing Teer to start up dinner.

They had a handful of the premixed stew packages his mother had sent him away with left, but they kept those for emergencies. The more Teer learned about himself, the more he suspected there was real magic in his mother's meal kits.

He could manage tossing dried vegetables and jerky into boiling water and adding a spice mix they'd bought from a store along the way. It was hard to put variety into their meals when *stew* was such an easy default, but Teer had been working on it—and he measured his success in the fact that Kard automatically set up to do dishes and let Teer cook.

"Thank you for coming here with me," he told the other man as he handed him a bowl of the stew. "We might be out of the way, but I know you don't like being this far west."

"If I get caught, *you* won't like it much either," Kard warned grimly. "I had to do what I did, but Taran also had to report it. She is bound, after all."

Kard, like most of the El-Spehari, had followed the Prince in Sunset into rebellion against the King in Winter. Teer's father had died in that war—in a battle where Kard had commanded the Sunset forces.

Taran, the El-Spehari commander of the Unity forces that had defended Shellsvan against the callipsuses, had been one of the few who *hadn't* joined the Prince in Sunset. Despite her loyalty through the rebellion, the Midnight Proclamation hadn't exempted her.

The King in Winter had declared that the El-Spehari would magically bind themselves to him or die. So, Taran was bound to the King she'd willingly served. Even when Kard had saved her life and many of the men under her command, that bond meant she'd been forced to try to bring him in.

Teer had knocked her out to protect Kard—though she'd *let* him. Abray's memories only made it clearer that he was no match for a fully trained Spehari in a straight fight.

Abray had, after all, been a Master of the Orders, one of the most powerful Adepts in his monastery, when the Spehari had betrayed them. He hadn't won that fight.

It would be turnings of careful work with the memories, teaching his muscles skills that Abray's had built over a lifetime, before he was even close to the strength of the dead man Storm had put in his head.

Teer swallowed a mouthful of the stew and smiled. It wasn't up to his mother's mixes yet, let alone her fresh stew, but he was getting better every time. Not a skill he'd expected to pull from the memories of an old Adept, but perhaps one that shouldn't have been a surprise in the memories of a hermit.

"Are we done here?" Kard repeated his question from earlier. "I don't want to rush you, but we are not as remote as you might think. The dragon lines run through Cossax, and the Wardkeeper will have received whatever orders are being passed."

"I…" Teer trailed off and looked down at his stew. "This is… harder than I like, Kard."

"Meaning?"

"I was about to say yes, now that we'd found Opal's grave, but now I think there's something else here." He looked up at the mountain to the west, the sun haloing the peak as it set. It would be a single-moon night, if he remembered correctly. Not enough light to keep searching.

"I need dawn—morning light, at least," Teer finally said as he managed to prod memories into some kind of shape. "I—*Abray* left something in a place that I'll need to use the shadows of the mountains to find.

"The other landmarks are long gone."

Kard nodded.

"Makes sense. We're here overnight anyway. Once we're on the roads, things will be less safe."

Teer considered something Kard had mentioned and the maps of the area they'd bought.

"What about the dragon lines?" he asked. "It would be… the North Green Line running through Cossax, right? That would end at Shiaray."

Kard paused, taking another bite of stew.

"I know that wasn't in Abray's memories," he pointed out. "Took *me* a minute. Yeah, the line would head east to Shiaray. What are you thinking?"

"Shiaray is where the cattle drives end," Teer said. If he'd been smarter and hadn't got drunk enough to take a potshot at a Spehari in full sight of everyone, he'd have been riding in those drives. It was a lucrative, if risky, career. One that could have seen him set up for his own ranch in a dozen turnings.

"I'm not clear how fast a dragon goes," he admitted, "but wouldn't we be faster taking one from Cossax out east? It would get us back into the frontier, the edge of the Unity, and we'd only have to worry about being recognized when getting aboard."

He glanced over at Star and Clack.

"Though the horses—"

"Would be just as fine as us," Kard interrupted. "Probably three days from Cossax to Shiaray. There might not be a dragon—or, at least, not with space—soon, but you're not wrong."

Teer didn't have the map memorized, but he held enough of it in his head to remember the riding time he'd been projecting. Somewhere between fifteen and twenty days, depending on the terrain and how swiftly the Latch Mountains smoothed out as they headed east.

A dragon could do that in three days? He'd know they could haul a lot of cargo, but that was far faster than he'd imagined! His idea was more useful than he'd thought.

"You usually use the same illusion to cover yourself in town," Teer said to Kard. "Can you appear as someone else?"

The El-Spehari grunted.

"Yeah. It's easier to just mask the most obvious Spehari parts of my features and still be *me*, but I can conjure an entire false face. Could make myself smaller or larger, too, but since I'm still *me* underneath, that gets obvious."

Teer glanced over at the other man. Both of them were tall with wide shoulders, enough so to stand out amongst most of the folk of the Unity. Teer hadn't met many Spehari in his life—if seeing the Magistrate on his once-a-turning visit to Alvid, the wardtown near the ranch he'd grown up on, counted.

They were tall but slim, which suggested that Kard owed his breadth and at least some of his height to his Merik mother.

"Nothin' else, that size won't make people think you're Spehari," Teer pointed out. "Hide your face and skin, people will look for another Merik like me."

"We'll draw some eyes no matter what. It's late in the turning for anyone to be heading east. The cattle drives are done till spring, at least. Fewer dragons will be running each way, and not many folk will be expected aboard in Cossax. The dragon'll stop there—they'll have orders to deliver—but they won't be expecting passengers."

"They'll take our money, but they'll look more than they might otherwise."

"Then we just have to look innocent as the snow," Teer replied. "Shouldn't be hard, after all."

It wasn't like they'd done anything wrong, really. The crime they were being hunted for was that Kard had *helped* the Unity—but so long as the last Lord Colonel of the Sunset Rebellion was at large, his mere existence was a crime.

And by both magic and choice, where Kard went, Teer went.

4

Teer woke to the smell of fresh bread and dark tea. Neither of those should have been on the campsite, and he opened his eyes to look up at a roof. That was *definitely* unexpected, and he reached for a gun as he rolled over—and off a bed, onto the floor.

The floor was covered in a handwoven rug. It wasn't a particularly *quality* handwoven rug, but Teer could remember Opal spending tendays slaving over the thing because she thought the bedroom floor was too cold.

With that, he knew where he was. He rose from the floor of Abray's bedroom, checking to confirm that he was still in his Hunter's duster and putting his hand on a gun underneath it.

The two quickshooters Teer wore were masterpieces of the gunsmiths' art, taken from a bounty hunter who'd refused to be talked down and drawn on Kard. The grip was familiar under his hand as he pushed the bedroom door open. Abray had never bothered to put a latch on it, but had set up the hinges to mostly swing closed on their own.

Teer was unsurprised to find the kitchen an exact match for his memories. A fire was burning in a stone hearth, heating both the pot of tea and the baking pan for the bread.

The sole occupant of the room was a stranger to him at first glance. The man was a touch paler than Teer but was definitely Merik, with shoulders even broader than the young Hunter's—but Teer towered head and shoulders over… Abray.

Even before Abray pulled the teapot off the hearth and turned to face him across the heavy wooden table, Teer realized who he was looking at. It was surprisingly difficult to recognize a man whose entire life was stored in his head—but how often did someone look at *themselves*?

"Teer. You're awake," the man greeted him. The accent would have been unfamiliar without their shared memories, but Teer recognized it as common in the region just to the north of the City of Pillars.

The region where the Spehari had first landed.

"I'm thinkin' I'm not, truly," Teer said carefully. "This house is gone, taken apart by friends of yours, and if I were awake, my friend would be here."

"Correct," Abray agreed. He poured two cups of tea and slid them onto the table. "A fact I took advantage of. I don't think Abray had this blend more than half a dozen times the turnings he lived here, but it is in the memories we share, so I could create it."

"Abray isn't in my head." Teer studied the two cups. Tea came from the north, originally a trade product with the Kott before the Prince in Sunset and his friends had rebelled. The Kott, a lizard-like race that lived in the swamps and jungles that marked the northern end of Unity territory, had joined that rebellion and never surrendered.

They were *still* at war, a fifteen-turning-long bloody drag on the Unity's resources. The Kott's too, Teer figured, but he had never met one of them. They didn't leave their swamps.

"Correct," Abray agreed again. "But there is a power in parallelism and synchronicity."

Teer stared blankly at the shorter man.

"If you want to talk, maybe use words I know?" he growled.

"You know them. Or you will. All I know is what's in your head now. All Abray ever was." Abray took a sip of the tea and closed his eyes in pleasure. "Short and simple, though. Abray's sense of self was tied up in this place. By resting here, you opened a link that allowed me to create, well, *this*."

He gestured around the house.

"And your actions here helped," he conceded. "Cleaning up Opal's grave. *Thinking* about who would have known the place was here to fix the marker, to take down the house respectful-like."

"*I* chose that," Teer said firmly.

"Correct," Abray repeated. "You chose things to respect Abray, his life, his home. Not because you shared his memories—though those memories guided you—but because you knew they were the right thing to do."

"If Abray isn't in my head, then you're not Abray," Teer noted. "Who *are* you?"

"Abray is… as close an approximation as you're going to find," the dream-figure admitted. As he spoke, though, a familiar scent wafted through the kitchen. The scent of air after a storm.

"You're not Storm, either." He wasn't certain of that, and he drew the gun in his hand, holding it on the table next to the tea. "But his scent is about you."

"Correct."

Teer was going to get sick of that word.

"I am a weapon, Teer," Abray told him flatly. "A creation of *the scent of air after the storm*'s, the trap inside his original offer and his final revenge if you somehow escaped. A revenge on Abray, too, in a sense."

"A weapon against me." Teer was glad he hadn't touched the tea. He'd learned some defenses against the callipsus's intrusions into his dreams from necessity, as Storm had tried to convince him to betray Kard.

"Correct. I was made to destroy you, Teer. To weaken your will so that you would lose yourself in our shared memory. Abray would rise from the ashes—but dead for all-too-many turnings, Abray has nothing to live for.

"He was a broken man before *the scent of air after the storm* killed him." Abray's image shrugged. "The expectation was that Abray would end himself and, with him, any last vestige of you."

"You're tellin' me this why?" Teer asked.

"Because for all that *the scent of air after the storm* had Abray's memories, the beast lacked much of the context to understand it. History, knowledge, culture... *being a Merik.* You understand our memories better than *the scent of air after the storm* did.

"And you know what the beast didn't. That you, like most Merik Adepts, are immune to magical mind control of any creature of this world."

Teer remembered his inner conflict against Storm and shivered.

"I resisted Storm's powers, but I was not *immune.*"

"The beast's illusions affected you, in a way that Spehari illusions would not, but they still failed against you," the construct told him. "But the true mental power of the beast simply failed upon you, as it failed upon Abray long ago.

"*The scent of air after the storm* was an old and arrogant creature. He believed that stealth and control would succeed where illusion and attack had failed. He was wrong."

Teer wasn't sure how much control either of them had of the dream, but his gun wasn't going anywhere, and it was trained on Abray.

"And this matters why?"

"Because *the scent of air after the storm* created a construct that required a fragment of an old Merik Adept's mind and then implanted it into the mind of *another* Adept." Abray grinned widely.

"I am not truly Abray," the construct concluded. "In a sense, *you* are more him than I am now, as you find a balance with his memories. I will not even endure forever. Unable and unwilling to complete my task, I will, in fact, fade away in a season at most. Nor, outside of a place of such synchronicity as this, will I be able to speak to you."

"But you wanted to."

"I did. Because while I only have Abray's memories through you, I *am* a tiny fraction of what he was beyond his memories. I needed to know what kind of man *the scent of air after the storm* had attempted to destroy."

"Do you like what you see?" Teer asked. "Am I to face your judgment now instead of the Courts of the Mounting Star's later?"

Abray took another swallow of the dream tea and shook his head.

"It is not a question of will I harm you, Teer," he offered. "I cannot. I am a construct of callipsus mind magic, and you are immune to any such harm I could attempt. I could block some of Abray's more critical memories from you, I suppose, but those blocks would not outlast me.

"What I could do is help you," he said. "There are prices to be paid for it, like any deal, but as I am more than Abray's memories, I can give you more than Abray's memories of his skills. I could spend my… essence to burn the memory of movement into your muscles, to turn half a century's worth of *knowledge* into half a century of *experience*."

Abray shrugged.

"It would not be a perfect process, and you will need to continue to practice and master the skills. Abray was rusty by the end, after all. That is part of why he died."

Teer considered the construct's words and implications.

"It would end you."

"Correct." The stranger smiled. "But I would guess my life at a season, maybe two. And you and I are what remains of the last Master Adept of the Merik Orders. Spending my essence in such a manner would give the world the first Adept of a new age.

"It would be worth it. *If* you were to be such an Adept."

"Which would be your price," Teer guessed.

"I am in your head, Teer," Abray's ghost reminded him. "No oath sworn falsely would matter. I must know, as only I could know, that you will walk the Adept's Path. Swear that oath and become what Abray failed to be."

That oath.

The words rang into Teer's mind unbidden. More than the words, the memory.

Abray kneeling in the center of the monastery training fields—mere yards, Teer realized, from where a Spehari Captain-Magistrate would strike him down turnings later—with a ring of raised metal fire around him and his companions.

There were five of them. They wore matching simple tunics of white cloth, and each carried a single sword, a straight, narrow-bladed weapon quite unlike the saber Kard had given Teer.

It was dusk, and a trio of older Adepts faced the graduating students. They wore the same simple white tunics, with heavy steel chains draped across their shoulders, the colors stark against black Merik skin in the firelight.

Like the novices, they wore swords on their belts, but opposite the blades they wore heavy pistols of a style unfamiliar to Teer.

The witnesses stepped forward across a silence broken only by the crackle of the fires, laying steel chains across the novices' shoulders to match their own. Watching through Abray's eyes, Teer could tell that the new chains were far simpler than those worn by the Masters.

"By this, my chain of steel," the five students intoned, the words flowing in a rough and ready unison, long practiced but never spoken in truth before that night. They touched the chains first, then lowered their hands to their swords.

"By this, my sword of iron." Their hands moved up to form fists over their hearts. "By these, the fires of my skill. I do swear upon my magic.

"I will keep my word unbroken.

"I will shield against the darkness.

"I will guard the innocent.

"I will uplift the humble.

"I will strike with only mercy.

"I will kill with only need.

"I will wield my magic true.

"I will strive to do no harm.

"I will teach those willing to swear this oath.

"This I swear upon my chain.

"This I swear upon my sword.

"This I swear upon my magic."

Teer *remembered* saying the words, but that was Abray's memory, a vivid image that faded as he shook his head and focused on the not-quite-dream around him.

"I have *always* tried to protect people," he protested. "You want an oath from me to prove that?"

"There is far more to that oath than just being a protector," Abray's ghost told him. "You know this in your heart. You walk the path of the hidden, chained to your companion by bonds of loyalty and magic, but so barred from being what you *should* be."

"I can't imagine that hangin' out a sign declarin' myself part of an order the Spehari destroyed a hundred turnings ago is conducive to my survival!"

"Correct and fair." Abray shrugged. "And that is not what I am asking of you. You must understand the oath, understand the path that an Adept should walk.

"We failed it." The stranger in Teer's dream seemed shadowed for a moment. "Some claimed we failed the moment we bent our knees to the Spehari, but there was little else we could do.

"What I am asking of you is not fair," Abray concluded. "I need you to succeed where hundreds like you failed. I need you to speak where we fell silent. To honor the oath that we broke.

"Someone must teach the Adepts to rise once more, but the massacre of those who came before means such a teacher will be an enemy to the Spehari and the Unity. I don't know if you can be that teacher while you walk with one of their children."

Teer had a moment of wondering whether the ghost-construct-*thing* in his head was as removed from his original supposed Storm-given mission as he claimed. Separating Teer and Kard would leave both of them weaker.

"I could not walk away from Kard without betrayin' promises and oaths that mean more to me than anythin' you could offer," Teer countered. "I could not break faith with him and *keep my word unbroken.*"

"You may one day have to choose." Abray shrugged. "For now, I ask you to consider the words of the oath. To consider the path of the

Adept, to remember what you can of the life Abray lived and the ideals he learned and tried to pass on.

"I was not a good teacher," he concluded with a sigh. "But I *was* a teacher. That knowledge lives in you now. Through you—and *only* through you—can the Adepts live again.

"From the memories alone, you can learn what an Adept should be. You can learn all that Abray was and become a Master in your own time. But if I help you, you will learn it far more quickly."

"At the price of betrayin' my friend."

"No." Abray shook his head. "At the price of becoming a true Adept, bound by our ancient oath and determined to resurrect the Merik Orders from the ashes. I do not know if that is a task that can be taken on alongside an El-Spehari. Such beings were few in my seasons."

"Either I am worthy or I am not," Teer told the being. "Swearin' your oath won't change that. You already don't believe I can be what you want of me, I'm thinkin'. Let me go."

"I believe that you *can* be what I want, Teer," Abray replied—the cottage slowly dissolving into mist around him. "I believe you understand what is holding you back.

"When you face it, you will choose. An oath will not matter."

The room dissolved into mist and Teer felt himself falling into a deeper slumber.

"When you are ready, I will be here," Abray's voice said from the shadows around him. "You will awake more refreshed than you might expect, and you will know the answer you couldn't remember last night. Consider it a gift and a reminder that this *did* happen."

5

Teer awoke for real as dawn began to edge around the mountains above them. Kard was on watch and had a pot of tea ready on the fire.

"You said there was something you'd need dawn to find?" Kard asked, gesturing around them. "It's not quite there, but the moons are gone, and the sun is rising. Good a time as any, if those memories are going to be useful."

Teer took a tea with grateful hands. He'd learned to be an easy riser chasing Harlon's herds across the ranch with the other hands, but he felt better than usual this morning.

He remembered the dream and Abray's promise, shaking it away as he sipped the tea. This was what he was used to, a heavy, over-brewed drink—utterly lacking in the scent of air after a storm.

"I can find it," he promised Kard, and realized that was true. The memory that had felt just beyond the edge of his mind the prior night was clear now, of Abray marking out steps along the shadow of the most southerly mountain to bury a chest where no one would think to dig.

He rose, the tea still in his hands, and pulled the folding shovel from their supplies. The memory wasn't clear enough for him to remember what was *in* the box, but it was enough for him to trace out Abray's steps.

Having seen the man now, if only in an odd dream-place, it was easy enough to adjust for the difference in their stride. He finished the last of his tea as he stared down at a patch of snow with nothing to distinguish it from the rest of the area around them.

"I'm not expecting another grave, so real digging today?" Kard asked, stepping up behind him with a shovel of his own. "I could make that easier."

"I'm not sure how well somethin' buried seventy turnings or more would survive your magic," Teer admitted. "Some chests can handle dirt; some can't. I don't think Abray knew he wasn't goin' to survive… though I don't guess he was plannin' to come back, either."

The dream conversation ran through his mind again, along with Storm's cold assumption that if Abray somehow won out over Teer in Teer's own head, the old Merik would have ended their shared life.

But if the memories were true, there was something beneath his feet. Even as he began to consider where to dig, the orange sparks of Kard's magic flared and the snow shifted aside, as it had done on the steps the previous day.

"I'll admit I was planning on digging all the way down, but I can move the *snow* without risking whatever Abray left you," the El-Spehari said. "I'll take your cup back while you take the first shift?"

"Thanks. We'll see how far down it is now," Teer said grimly.

———

BOTH THE MAN who had buried the chest and the man digging it up were stronger and faster than most others. Abray had buried it a yard beneath the soil. Time had added another half a dozen inches of dirt from one source or another, but Teer's measurement had been perfect.

He hadn't been *sure* of that, of course, and he'd been about to start expanding the hole rather than going deeper when the blade of the shovel hit wood.

Kard heard it as well as he did, the El-Spehari standing at the edge of the hip-high hole.

"That didn't sound like a root," he observed. "*Now* can I use magic instead of a shovel?"

Between Teer's physical gifts and Kard's magical earth-moving, they exposed the chest in short order after that. It was a large iron-bound box, four feet long by two wide and two high.

It was large enough that getting it out of the hole was awkward, taking both of them working together. Even Teer had started considering a pulley before they finally had it on the ground.

"Not even locked," Kard said. "Though I suppose if no one else knows where you buried it, that's probably good enough."

"Abray didn't *have* any locks," Teer pointed out. Abray could make a lot of things, but he'd needed to get metalwork from Cossax. There'd been a few clever latches around the house that had required tricks to open, but there'd been no real locks.

Time had done more to secure the chest than any lock, and it took careful use of Teer's carving knife to open the latch and throw back the lid.

"Lined with oiled leather," Kard said approvingly. "Anything less might not have survived up here. This soil isn't dry enough for burying something to work well."

Teer wasn't paying any attention to the box itself. The contents were each individually wrapped with leather that crinkled to the touch with waterproofing waxing. All of the packages were bulky things, but it was unclear how much of that was the leather itself.

The first unwrapped surprisingly easily as he pulled on it. A familiar metal weapon revealed itself, though Teer hadn't seen a pistol like it before. It was bigger than the quickshooters he was used to but lacked the cylinder that allowed the gun to fire five shots without reloading.

"I haven't seen one of these in a while," Kard said, looking down at the gun. "Heavy bastards. Thought was that if you only got one shot, you should make it worth it.

"A proper hunter or repeater will do you more good against most targets, but…" The El-Spehari ran his fingers over the gun and flipped up a block to reveal the chamber. "Heavy slug, heavy powder charge. I'd use any quickshooter over it, but when I first served the Unity, these were the pistols we issued."

And they were the pistols the Master Adepts had carried in Abray's memory, Teer realized. Like Kard, Abray had likely been issued the gun by the Unity.

"I don't see any ammunition," he told Kard. "And I doubt it's in good enough shape to use over quickshooters, as you say. Guess he didn't take it with him."

Teer had a solid memory of the weapons Abray had taken with him to hunt Storm. A thunderbuss, a pellet-firing weapon that had changed little since Abray's death. A spear with a heavy steel head and crossbar, designed to fight bears and other heavy, aggressive wildlife. A bow of a kind Teer had no familiarity with—and the bow was what Abray had taken Storm's eye with.

The old Adept had expected taking a two-foot-long arrow with a steel tip to the skull would kill the big lizard. He'd been wrong, and the callipsus had killed him in turn—but from the conversations with Captain-Magistrate Taran, *Spehari* had gone after Storm and left less mark on the callipsus.

From that thought, though, Teer knew what the next package was even before he unwrapped it. The bow inside was deceptively small, barely over a yard long, and the curve was inverted from how it would sit when strung.

Looking at it, he could see the carefully connected layers of bone and sinew and wood, each adding their own piece to a draw weight that even Kard would fail to draw without magic. A second package had been tucked inside the leather holding the bow, wax and parchment, and more leather wrapped around what he knew would be three bowstrings.

Even stored like that, Abray's memories told him that the strings would be dangerous to use. It would be safer to make new strings—and the memory of how to do so was also in his mind.

He shook his head to clear the vagaries and saw Kard looking at the seemingly backward bow with a confused gaze.

"It'll take both of us to string this," he told the other man. "Abray could put a shaft on target every few heartbeats with it, each one fit to go through a man and into the next."

"You told me he hit Storm with his bow. So... which bow is this one?"

"His first bow," Teer replied. "He was in good shape, but he wasn't as strong at the end as he was when he arrived here in the mountains. He made this one in training, used it in Unity service and brought it with him when he ran."

"The draw grew too heavy for him, so he made himself a new bow he could wield."

"A bow that put an arrow through Storm's eye," Kard observed. "And that was his *easy* bow."

"Aye."

There was a wary respect in Teer's mentor's gaze now. "Any arrows?"

"Like the strings, they're not usable," Teer replied, pulling another leather-wrapped package out and unfolding it to reveal a quiver with two dozen shafts. "Some might be okay, I'll go through 'em later, but I'll detach most of the heads and make new arrows."

He knew without even looking that there were two types of arrowheads in the quiver: sharp-pointed piercing arrows that would go through any armor he'd ever seen, and wider broadheads, designed to take down unarmored targets with brutal internal damage.

"You've got a repeater and a hunter," Kard pointed out. "Is a bow really useful?"

"For most, no," Teer conceded. "For me? I can hit almost as hard with this as with a quickshooter, at ranges more like those of the hunter... and completely silently."

"Point. What's the big one?" His friend's gesture indicated a long, narrow package at the bottom of the chest.

There were other packages, smaller ones, other things that Abray hadn't wanted to take with him and couldn't risk being found. One would be ammunition for the single-shot pistol he hadn't seen at first —only as useful as the obsolete weapon itself. Several others contained money, though between bounties and loot, even their recent spate of running without work hadn't dented Teer's purse too badly.

Six, he knew without counting, held books that Abray had salvaged from the monastery's library after the fire. None were undamaged, but the old Adept had preserved them carefully and repaired what he could. They would be of immense value, especially if Teer decided to follow the path the ghost in his mind wanted him to and started trying to teach.

The big package, though, had clearly defined the length of the chest. Everything else had been added later, but Teer suddenly knew that the chest had been made to hold *this*.

The wrapping on it was older and stiffer. It had been rewaxed repeatedly, to make certain it remained secure against the weather and moisture, but it slowly peeled away under Teer's hands.

He heard Kard's shocked inhalation as the sword revealed itself, but put that aside, letting the memory of the blade return to him. He wasn't sure what had kept those memories of Abray's from him before, but as he drew the weapon from the plain scabbard, they came in a rush.

From pommel to tip, the sword was four feet long. Three feet of that was the blade, straight and sharp as a razor. Unlike the saber Kard had given him, the sword's blade had two edges, narrowing to a point as sharp as any of the arrows—and that blade was pitch-black, seeming to absorb the light of the mountain valley around them.

There were no delicate waves of a complex alloying process like those that marked the Kott-steel saber. It was one smooth and uniform piece of a strange metal from hilt to tip. The guard was a different metal, paler than the blade despite the use of black enamel by the smith to minimize the difference.

The hilt had been wrapped in a leather he'd never seen, almost black without any dye and with a rougher texture and better grip than any animal hide he'd seen before. Even Abray's memories didn't tell him what the hide was—the sword had come into his hands like this, and the only work he'd ever done was carefully sharpening the blade.

The hilt was long enough for him to put both hands on it, with the heavy pommel of black-enameled iron large enough that he could grip it as well. Instinct placed his hands on the sword—left just below the guard, right on the pommel.

This was the type of blade Abray had trained with. More, Teer knew that this particular sword was important, critical even, to the man who'd buried it.

"Teer," Kard said in a warning tone. "That is a *black-iron sword*. By the Iron Pillars, who *was* Abray?"

"The last Master Adept of the Order of the Black Blade," Teer replied. He hadn't remembered the name of Abray's specific order until that moment, another thing in his memories that had been protected... by the blade's own power?

"His order was named for this sword," he continued. "A gift from the Spehari for loyal service. Wielded by a chosen champion—*not* Abray, but the woman was there when the Spehari came for them."

"Abray was left for dead and took the blade from her body while the monastery burned."

Along with the books. Teer sheathed the blade, unconsciously following memories of Abray's motions and slinging the scabbard over his shoulder. He unwrapped the books as Kard tried to find words to explain what they had just found.

"I suppose the simplest thing I can say, my young friend, is that you have found something the King in Winter wants more than me," Kard finally told him.

Teer paused, looking down at the hand-tooled cover of the book in his hand. Abray had replaced the covers on all of the books; he had no idea which of the texts it contained.

"What do you mean?" he asked.

"When the Spehari arrived, the only iron in Aran came from the Kott," his friend explained. "The Merik had tin, copper and bronze.

Trade had brought a few iron tools and swords down from the north, but our people fought with arrows and bronze spears. Looking at that bow, I finally believe some of the stories I was told about Merik archers, but the Spehari couldn't build muskets, let alone true hunters and repeaters, with bronze.

"They needed iron, so they broke down the ships that had brought them here. Some of it went into the first Iron Pillars, but the rest went into a variety of things they needed. Tools, guns... swords.

"I don't know what's unique about the black iron of those ships," Kard admitted. "I know the Spehari can't make more. I'm not sure if it's a lost art or something about crossing the Nightmare Sea from the west that changed those ships.

"I *do* know that every scrap of black iron the King in Winter could find was reclaimed. Most to go into the Iron Pillars, I believe, but I suspect the old bastard had other uses for it." He looked at the sword hung over Teer's shoulder with discomfited eyes.

"I have seen a black-iron sword before. My father carried it in the King in Winter's service when I was very young—the last, so far as I knew, to ever exist. He surrendered it to the King sixty turnings ago.

"In exchange for a protective armlet forged by the King's own hand and charged with a portion of the King's own divine power. *That* is what a black-iron blade is worth, Teer. A portion of the King in Winter's strength bound forever."

"Should you carry it, then?" Teer asked. The part of him shaped by Abray's memories rebelled, but he'd expected that and resisted it.

He finished unwrapping the books as Kard considered. Only one still had its original cover, with a faded inlay marking the title as *Magic Before the Landing, the Skills of the Merik.*

Of the books Abray had left him, it was probably the least immediately practical and yet, in some ways, the most important. *Magic Before the Landing* wouldn't contain any of the rituals or training manuals or diagrams or, well, anything he could use to learn his powers.

But it would explain what the Merik Adepts *thought* about their powers, where they came from and what their limits might be.

"I can't carry black iron," Kard finally told him. "I don't think I could resist the temptation to channel power through the blade, which would augment my spells threefold in power. And from some of the tasks I carried out for the King in the past, I believe he can sense any use of black iron for that purpose.

"If he could sense black iron just sitting there, well, Abray couldn't have hidden in exile," the El-Spehari warned grimly. "It should be safe for you to wield it as a blade, and it might be safe for you to let it work on your magic, but I fear that if I touch that sword, the King in Winter will know where it is.

"Possibly even *who* touched it, which would see my father sent on the hunt."

And Kard's father was the Lord Inquisitor Akane, the Spehari charged above all others to bring the rogue children of the Unity's masters to heel.

"I need the books, the bow and the sword," Teer said quietly. "The money we can probably use, but the gun is useless. If I knew where he fell, I'd bury it with him, but even if I could find the spot…"

Abray's bones would be long gone. Storm wouldn't have buried the man; he'd have left the corpse where it fell, and nature would have handled the rest.

"Let's pack everything up," Kard agreed. "Then let's get heading down to Cossax."

He looked around the valley.

"This whole place feels like it should be a memorial to the couple who lived and loved here," he admitted. "We needed to come here, to see it and to find what Abray had left behind, but I feel like we're intruding."

"I think this"—Teer gestured at the books, bow and sword—"Abray would have wanted me to find. With it, I could train other Adepts."

He chuckled.

"Once I know how to find 'em, anyway."

"And figure out how to hide that from the Unity," Kard growled.

"The same time we hid the people you decided weren't going to get justice in the Unity," Teer countered. "East of their territory, working with the tribes they haven't subjugated yet. I might have to find students in the Unity, but I don't need to *teach* 'em under Spehari eyes."

Ever since Shellsvan, Kard had been more and more determined to hide. Teer didn't disagree, but while he'd originally signed on with the El-Spehari to save his life, he'd stayed because they were helping people.

If all they did was hide, who were they helping?

6

Dusk was beginning to fall when the pair finally rode onto something that resembled an actual road. Like most such in the Unity, it was maintained by the Unity Army, and whatever snow had fallen on it had been cleared away.

That left a smooth stone surface ten yards wide, designed for marching boots. Wagons and horses would benefit from the road as well, but Teer knew—both from cynical commentary from Kard and Abray's memories—that the Unity's main roads were built for infantry.

Originally almost all Merik, now a mix of all the various races the Unity ruled, those infantry were the heart of the Army, regiments a thousand strong that would march these roads in columns five wide.

Five regiments to a brigade. Twenty-six such brigades had followed the Prince in Sunset into rebellion, giving his army the name *the Sunset Brigades*—though by the end of the Sunset Rebellion, Teer understood that at least twice that many soldiers had served under El-Spehari like his friend.

"Where does this even lead?" he asked Kard. "I would expect it to run alongside the dragon line."

"It's older," Kard explained. "The road has to be wider than the dragon line, so they built them in flatter areas. Even with magic and explosives, they can only make a ten-yard-wide path so straight through the mountains."

He pointed up ahead of them. Following his gesture, Teer saw a vague mark on the mountains north of them. If he hadn't been looking for it, he might not have noticed it—but now that he'd seen it, he couldn't mistake that blade-straight line for anything natural.

"But soldiers can turn easily compared to a dragon," he said. "That has to go straight or turn slowly, even with the lines to run along. They go higher to go straighter. Plus, it keeps the lines safe from rebels and troublemakers. The mountain lines are hard to fix—but the only way to *reach* them is by the line itself."

"But the road meets the dragon line at Cossax," Teer remembered from the map. "So, the straight path and the flat path are close there?"

"Without proper survey maps, I can't be sure, though I know we'd have given up some perfection on the dragon line to bring it into an existing town." Kard shrugged. "Plus, Cossax is located at a central point in the passes; that's why it exists at all."

It had started from an inn, Teer recalled. An inn they weren't going to reach before dark.

"We're still a quarter-day's ride from the town," he warned. "Sun's already setting and it's only one moon again tonight. We should camp soon."

"Yeah." Kard looked around. "Won't be any spaces built for it, but there should be some clear ground around. Let's get back from the road. Just in case."

Teer nodded. Despite everything, he *understood* Kard's concern about the nation they stood in. The Unity would kill Kard if they caught him, and while Teer was reasonably sure he could survive whatever their magical bond would do to him when the other man died, he doubted the Unity would let him walk away.

Still, something about the shadowy mountain forest along the side of the road worried him.

———

SNOW DROPPED from an evergreen as Teer pulled Star up and brushed a branch. The forest was sparse enough that they could ride—carefully—but between twilight and trees, it was becoming unwise, and they hadn't found anywhere clear enough to camp for the night.

"We're going to have to just tuck against some trees and settle," Kard declared, pulling Clack up next to him. "I'd hoped for space for a fire, but I think we're at roadtack and bedrolls to get through the night. At least we know there's a hotel waiting for us in the morning."

Teer nodded silently, but it was more than the dip of the sun behind the mountains that had stopped him. He held up a hand as Kard started to speak.

"We're being hunted," he told the Hunter, a shiver running down his spine as he realized the certainty of his words.

There might have been snow up there in the Latch Mountains, but it wasn't truly winter yet. Even there, there were birds going about the motions of the last tenday or so of their safe season, stockpiling food and reinforcing nests.

The silence hadn't settled in until after they'd left the road. Everything in the woods was holding its breath, waiting to see what happened next.

Kard held up his hand, four fingers up, then folded down two of them.

Four legs or two.

Teer held up his own hand in a matching gesture, holding up four fingers as his sharpened senses reached out into the darkness. Unlike regular two-legged prey, he and Kard could see in the dark—but he would *hear* wolfen or something like the venomous canids before he saw them.

He reached back to draw his hunter. The long breechloading rifle was a gift from his mother's husband. Hardin had contributed to the emotional catastrophe that had ended in Teer trying to shoot Kard, and the man had felt like Teer's new status—forced to leave home and legally Kard's property—was his fault.

So, he'd given Teer the best gun he owned, the one he'd carried as a cattle-drive outrider. It was a gorgeous weapon of blued steel with one of the few telescopic optics Teer had seen in his life.

He wasn't going to use the optics tonight—but it was also the gun he carried that fired the heaviest and most powerful bullets. Somehow, he knew he was going to need that.

Star whinnied softly, but before Teer could even whisper to the horse, Clack shouldered her. There was no force to the gelding's touch, but it was enough to warn the mare that she needed to be quiet.

Star was a rancher's horse, strong enough, fast enough and enduring enough to act as a Hunter's mount. Clack was a *warhorse*— and given that the Sunset Rebellion had been sixteen turnings earlier, Teer had to wonder where Kard had found him.

Something moved. Something *very* stealthy, stealthier than Teer had expected, and he turned in the saddle as quietly as he could. He listened to the movement and lifted two fingers where he knew Kard could see.

Two creatures. Too quiet to be wolfen—the monsters were soft-pawed and naturally sneaky but not like *this*. He couldn't aim by the sound, and he couldn't even tell how far away they were.

Kard seemed to have the same reaction. Dark sparks of magic flickered around the El-Spehari, fluttering through the trees like the missing birds, trying to find their hunters.

He could see his companion's magic, but he wasn't hearing whatever it was telling Kard. Teer could *see* but he was still blind.

And then it was too late. He saw movement, barely a blur of shadow in the twilit forest. There wasn't even a change in color, the creature blending in so well that it was almost invisible.

Teer moved with Star, pulling the mare to the side and touching his heels to her flanks to urge her into a run. She had scented something and leapt forward with a will—and the leaping strike hit the snow in a visible burst of white debris.

The creature was still a blur, but its size was clear now—whatever it was, it matched Star in size and was *far* less friendly.

It took Teer less than a moment to slip out of his saddle, his own impact far louder than the strange creature hunting him. He had a vague sense of it raising itself from the snow, shaking its head at him —and a spark of familiar pain hit his head.

Illusion magic. Like the callipsuses they'd fought at Shellsvan and before, this creature was drawing on natural power to hide itself.

He raised the hunter, forcing himself to see past the shroud the creature gathered around itself, and pulled the trigger as the beast began to charge.

Teer hadn't missed an unrushed shot in turnings, if ever, and his eye didn't fail him. The creature emerged from the shadow, a mix of the dusk and its own magic, and his shot took it in the eye.

The hit didn't stop the creature's leap and it slammed into him, forcing him to drop the hunter as teeth as long as his hand snapped at his face.

With the magic broken, he saw that it was a white-furred beast, moving on four legs as thick as his own torso. Ugly claws tipped those limbs, and the beast rolled away from him, coming silently back up onto its hind paws and lashing out at him with the claws.

Teeth and claws alike were black and dangerous, and while Teer might not have been able to *name* the creature, he realized that it didn't really want to fight him. It wanted to eat his horse, and he was simply in the way.

Teer wasn't going to give Star up to it, and he knew it would happily add his body to the meal. Silent as it was, the creature was still moving, but the eye he'd hit was gone, weeping blood from a wound he wasn't sure the thing would survive.

He dodged back from swiping claws and gnashing teeth, trying desperately to draw one of his guns. The *bear*—Abray's memories threw up the name, though Abray hadn't known this particular breed —closed, moving fast. Faster than any animal should, but not enough to outmatch Teer.

Enough to keep him moving, slowing his attempt to draw a quick-shooter. He finally got the weapon clear as the bear made the sound he'd heard from it, a tearing growl of frustration as it tried to jump on him and push him to the ground.

Teer stepped into its charge, slamming his shoulder into the beast's chest and holding up its entire immense weight for a few seconds.

Enough seconds to place his quickshooter against its throat and put five heavy bullets upward into its head. It continued to push down on him, muscle and weight working together, for another few seconds before it suddenly went limp.

He pushed the weight aside, listening with all his might to try to locate the other bear—and Kard and the horses!

A familiar heart-wrenching scream tore through the forest, and Teer's breath caught in his throat. He started running toward it without thinking—not even sure *which* horse was screaming, but knowing that the poor working animals didn't deserve the messes people pulled them into.

The small pain of illusion magic struck him again and he pushed through it, relying on his hearing to pick up the bear's surprisingly stealthy movements—a focus that *hurt* when the horse screamed again.

Then he burst into a small gap in the trees, where Clack was on the ground in a manner that Teer knew no horse could manage on its own—and Kard was kneeling next to the horse, facing away from it with a Kott-steel saber in his hand and a glow of dark red power covering them both.

Except that Teer could see the bear and Kard couldn't. It had moved back from them and was coming from the side, away from Kard and his shield.

Teer hadn't had time to reload the gun he'd drawn and didn't have *time* to draw the other. The beast was already moving in, unseen to its prey, and if Clack was possibly already dead, Kard was upright.

Teer leapt. The bear did the same in the same moment, and Teer would never have been able to tell anyone if he'd known the creature was about to leap or if he was just getting in the way.

The gun fell from his hand. He barely realized he'd dropped it.

He *did* realize he'd drawn the black-iron sword. He'd drilled with a Kott-steel saber, but it had never felt quite right for Abray's drills. *This* sword fit those drills to the point where it didn't matter that he was in the air and about to collide with a beast ten times his own weight.

He moved in the air, the sword whistling around in a manner his hindbrain wasn't entirely convinced was possible, and collided with the bear blade-first. The black iron sank deep into its flank, slicing through flesh and fur with disturbing ease before lodging itself in bone as Teer impacted the creature.

Unlike its companion, this bear never made a sound before it hit the ground. Teer landed on top of it, and something in how it gave beneath him told him it was dead.

The forest was silent around him. That was bad. He couldn't hear Star or Clack… or *Kard*, who was only a few yards away.

Teer pulled himself to his feet, surprised to find himself dizzy and unsteady like he'd missed eating for a day. He shook his head, closing his eyes, and felt some of his balance return. Clack was still and silent on the snow, but Kard was upright.

The El-Spehari was still kneeling. He'd dropped the shield of his magic—but he'd also dropped the saber and was staring at Teer blankly, his eyes strangely wide and vacant.

"Kard?" Teer demanded. "Kard?!"

His friend blinked, slowly. He was clutching his stomach, and small sparks of white magic seemed to be *trying* to form around his hands.

Then he collapsed forward into the snow and Teer knew he was in serious trouble.

7

From Abray's memories, Teer had learned how to heal his own injuries with surprising effectiveness. He knew that Kard's magic could heal both the user and others, but the Adept powers he was mastering couldn't.

Which made it a problem when Kard was the one down, his guts revealed by a claw strike that had cut under his Hunter coat. Something in the smell and color hit a memory of Abray's, not enough to *help* but enough for him to know that the bear's claws were venomous.

Worse, Clack was gone. The big, loyal warhorse had been *too* loyal, following Kard's instructions to escape the bears until he'd hit a root and broken a foreleg. With Kard around, the horse could have been saved—except that the bears had been hunting the horses first. Once down, Clack hadn't stood a chance.

Teer had no horses, a dying companion who was the only one with magic that could heal someone else and the handful of supplies he had on him. He'd dropped one of his quickshooters *and* his stepfather's hunter.

It was dark. It was cold. He was alone. And if he did nothing and gave in to that, Kard was going to die.

The part of him that carried Abray's anger whispered to let

him die. The part of him that carried *both* of their anger knew that letting Kard die would serve the Unity and the King in Winter.

That reminder let him focus the anger.

He'd moved Kard enough to get his friend laid out on his back. It wasn't the best position for most injuries, but a gut wound wasn't most injuries. He could see the darkness beginning to seep through the quick bandaging job he'd done, and shivered at more than the cold.

He'd been badly injured a couple of times in Kard's service, but between the El-Spehari's magic and the occasional help of Kotan shamans of their acquaintance, he'd been able to bounce back quickly enough that no one had even realized he was healing faster than naturally on his own.

Teer blinked.

Kotan shamans. His first serious injury had been treated by a failed trainee shaman named Doka. All Doka had used were poultices, herbal mixtures that she said were enhanced by being applied by a shaman but would work for anyone.

And they had several of those poultices among their supplies. Supplies that were tucked away in poor Clack's saddlebags.

Swallowing grimly, Teer crossed to the dead horse. He took a moment to close the gelding's wide eyes, a gesture he hoped would help the poor loyal beast's spirit, and then started to remove the saddlebags.

As he worked through the bags, he felt the inexplicable urge to do *more* for the dead horse, and the words stumbled from his lips without much thought.

"Clack, warhorse and brave companion," he said to the night. "I will commit your body to the soil, I promise, knowing your spirit has left for the Courts of the Mounting Star. May my words follow your spirits and weigh upon your final Judgments.

"May the Magistrates of the Mounting Star know that you died protecting a friend. My words cannot judge your life, but I knew your strength and your honor, and that your loyalty was beyond question.

May They understand the fate that befell you and show you mercy in those most ancient Courts."

He'd once heard Kard give the Charge of the Final Judgment and been surprised that the El-Spehari knew all the words. Now, thanks to Abray's memories, so did he.

And if he'd just said those words over a horse, well, Clack had been Kard's loyal companion for far longer than Teer. The gelding's spirit deserved to know he was remembered.

———

TEER HAD ALWAYS SUSPECTED that Kard's saddlebags were larger on the inside than the outside, just because of the other Hunter's ability to continually produce all sorts of tools and weapons from inside. He had *known*, for example, that there were two spare Kott-steel sabers somewhere in Clack's saddlebags.

Spreading out Kard's gear across an impromptu campsite and searching for supplies he knew were in there told him he'd underestimated just how *much* larger the saddlebags were.

He kept things neatly organized, but he not only found the two spare sabers, he also found no less than *four* spare short repeaters—the specialty rapid-fire weapons used by Unity cavalry that had become symbolic of the Sunset Rebellion—along with two hunters and a dozen quickshooters of various makes and ages.

Teer recognized most of the weapons as the ones they'd taken from a party of Hunters who'd realized that Kard was smuggling a selection of his bounty targets to safety, but there were definitely weapons in the bags he'd never seen before.

He knew where all of the camping supplies were—those weren't really in the saddlebags, since they often required specific carrying cases for things like the folding cauldron and campfire tripod—and had put those aside first. He'd figured he knew which bag had the spare swords, so he'd checked it first to eliminate it.

The second bag he checked had books, only about half of them written in languages Teer *recognized*, let alone could read. A few twinges of recognition from Abray's memories suggested he could work through them if he needed to, but since he also saw journals and letters, he simply stacked them back into the saddlebag and moved on.

The third bag had a wide variety of miscellaneous supplies, including an entire backup set of every single piece of camping gear that the two of them had split across their horses *outside* of Kard's impossible saddlebags.

Including, he noted, no less than four bedrolls. All brand-new, with Unity Army tags suggesting Kard had acquired them from the quartermasters in Shellsvan either before the final callipsus attack or while Teer had been distracted healing during their final flight from their temporary allies.

With all of the camping gear and weapons that Kard carried mounted on his saddle, there only *were* five saddlebags, and Teer was surprised to realize the fourth appeared to be entirely nonmagical. It contained a heavy purse and several leather folios of paper.

Despite the need, everything had already taken long enough that Teer gave in to his curiosity and opened one of the folios. It contained bank ledgers, each under a different name, for accounts with different banks and merchant houses. Each, if taken to the right location of the bank or company in question, would allow for the withdrawal of stamped redcrystal stones or glass shards from the account.

The folio he was looking at held at least two dozen ledgers, and the smallest said that a man named Alekdon had deposited the sum of eighty-two stones, seventy-eight shards, with the West Orange Line Dragon Company.

That was a third of what Hardin's ranch brought in over an entire turning—and unlike those stones, this wasn't money to be eaten by costs and paying hands. This was just sitting on the books of a dragon line company far in the west, one that Teer suspected Kard would never be near again.

If the other folios were similar, Kard had more money than Kard had ever imagined. He'd been surprised when the other man had given him a quarter of the payment for their first bounty, and now he began to understand.

Though he had to wonder how many of the accounts were, like West Orange Dragon Line, in places where Kard would never be able to access them again.

Shaking that away, Teer grabbed the last bag and basically upended it onto the tent cloth he'd spread out for organizing. While the saddlebag contained several objects he couldn't identify—most involving redcrystal in a form other than coinage—the medical supplies were carefully split out and clearly organized.

The Kotan poultices had been at the bottom of the bag, but dumping them out left them easily found—and since Teer suspected Doka's care was the only reason he could still use his arm, he remembered clearly what they looked like.

Taking the wax-sealed cloth packages, he returned to where he had a lean-to set up over Kard. He should have started a fire, he realized, but a quick touch told him that Kard was burning up. The venom was working its way through his blood, and there was a strange, sickly purple tint to his pale skin.

The smell might not have triggered anything solid from his stolen memories, but that did. Days of Abray sitting over Opal as she struggled against wolfen venom ran through his head, and he realized that whatever the bear's poison was, it was closely related to the one carried by the wolflike predators.

That gave him another starting point. First, though, he had to stop a gut wound from killing his friend.

He peeled away the bandages carefully, grimacing at the amount of blood. There was no obvious smell of pus or shit, though, which suggested that the claw hadn't torn as deeply as he'd feared.

Carefully, Teer removed the wax from the Kotan poultice. A strong scent of various herbs he couldn't identify wafted out, and he hoped he was doing it right. He tried to focus some of the fire that burned inside him into the medicine, but he doubted his magic was the right type.

Still. He knew from his own experience that the poultice would fight infection and help heal the wound quickly. He pressed it into the wound, mouthing a silent apology to his friend as he guessed how much that would hurt if Kard was awake, then wrapped fresh bandages around the poultice and the injury.

Exhaustion swept over him and he pushed it back. The Kotan poultice would help with the poison, but it was a broad magic. Because it would help with any potential injury, it could not fully counteract the poison.

But Abray's memories contained the recipe for a draught that could. Or, at least, it counteracted *wolfen* poison, which seemed to work in much the same way.

Some of the ingredients, he could gather in the area even in late fall and early winter. Others would be harder, but they were things that Kard should have in the medical supplies.

At least one *needed* to be found at night. For a moment, Teer wished he had Doka with him—or even Lora, the young woman they'd captured for her bounty and then delivered to the Kota for safety when they'd learned the truth behind her crimes. Lora had been a townswoman, and aspects of long-distance travel had worn on her —but she could have at least stood watch while Teer went hunting for flowers.

And, well, his horse and his stepfather's gun. There were a lot of things lost in the night, and only the soft sounds of distant wildlife gave Teer any confidence that he was safe to leave Kard alone.

That life had been missing prior to the attack by the strange bears. Its presence now, he hoped, meant that there was nothing *else* hunting the dark night.

8

"*H*ullo, de camp!"

Teer started awake, grasping for the hunter laid across his lap. From the state of the campfire, he hadn't been asleep that long—a good thing, since he hadn't meant to fall asleep.

He'd been awake through the entire night, though. Thanks to the Courts, Star had wandered out of the twilight while he'd been hunting for the herbs for the antivenom draught. He'd found everything he needed to and started the draught simmering on the fire when he'd sat down.

And then, apparently, fallen sufficiently asleep that someone could approach the camp without waking him up.

"Who's there?" he snapped, rising to his feet with the long gun trained in the direction of the sound.

"Jus' a passerby, saw de fire and wonder who would be camped up round midday!" An unclear figure stepped into Teer's view, though it took him a minute to realize that the fuzziness around the man wasn't his eyes.

It was the way the man was dressed. He wore multiple layers of furs, and his hair was long and uneven. There were ties in the hair to keep it mostly organized, but the chaos of the furs meant the stranger gave the impression of wild hair no matter what.

He had his hands in the air, clearly seeing Teer's gun.

"Things good here?" he asked, taking in the haphazard camp and the rough lean-to arranged over Kard's unconscious form.

Keeping an eye on the stranger, Teer checked the pot on the stove. It hadn't boiled over, thankfully, and it was only approaching a pale pink color. The recipe he remembered said it would be red when it was ready.

"We were attacked by strange beasts last night," Teer said grimly. "There may be more. Big white things, killed my friend's horse and injured him before we took 'em down."

The stranger glanced around.

"Wolfen get white in winter," he said. "They've a nasty bite."

"I know wolfen," Teer said shortly. He still had the gun trained near the man, if not right on him. "These were bigger. Nastier, hard to see in the dark."

He shook his head.

"No harm, traveler, but I've an injured friend I need to treat and then two horses' worth of gear and men to get to town on one," he told the stranger. "Might be best if you were movin' on."

The other traveler shifted and much of his apparent bulk vanished. Teer realized that the furs he'd thought the man was wearing were on a frame he'd been carrying over his shoulders. Underneath the man's catch was a surprisingly thin figure in a simpler coat—still fur, but rather roughly made. Even though he'd clearly been outside for a while, the skin Teer could see past the hair and beard was paler than his own, more the color of parchment.

A Zeeanan, then—which made sense, since they were in the old territory of that tribe.

"Name's Shill," he said brightly. "Trap and hunt in dese mountains. Know the beasts pret' well. Wan' to take a look at de beast?"

That seemed harmless enough, and Teer could see his draught beginning to darken further.

He waved in the direction of the bodies.

"One that way about twenty yards, the other maybe two hundred beyond that," he told Shill. "I'm more worried about my friend than the furs, if you want 'em."

Shill gave him a deep nod and then strode off into the trees—though his carrying frame remained on the edge of the campsite, warning Teer he was coming back.

Which was a problem, because the last Teer needed was for a random trapper to realize Kard was El-Spehari!

———

However few minutes of sleep Teer had managed between falling asleep watching the fire and being woken up by Shill's arrival, it was enough to stave off the sharp edge of exhaustion. He checked on Kard as the draught simmered toward completion.

The strange tint to his skin was still there. It was getting stronger, though Kard's breathing remained strong, and he wasn't waking up.

Teer checked the bandages around his friend's stomach. Nothing had seeped through this time, which was promising. He wasn't sure how long to wait before switching the Kotan poultices, but thanks to the generosity of the tribe they'd stayed with last, they had a full dozen of them.

Doka had swapped his every day, he recalled, but he figured that swapping sooner the first day was a good plan. They had the wraps to spare if he was wrong, at least.

Getting Kard to drink the draught was a struggle. At no point did the big man wake up, forcing Teer to prop the other man half-upright on his knees, open his mouth with one hand, and then pour the liquid in with the other.

From what he remembered of the recipe, he got enough in to help, though the completely unconscious coughing fit that followed worried him.

This time, he laid Kard back down in a safer position for his breathing, on his side with a knee and an arm out in front to prop him up. That would keep him breathing clearly if the coughing returned, but as Teer got him settled, he could feel a slight relaxation in the tensed muscles.

It might have been just hope, but it looked like the purple tint was already fading a bit.

Teer turned back to the pot he'd pulled off the stove and went through the pile of gear for a canteen. He poured out the water into a jug—no sense wasting it, even with snow around—and then filled the canteen with the draught he'd made.

He had five more doses and enough ingredients to make a second batch. Against wolfen poison, it could take as much as half a dozen doses over three days to break the fever—and Teer suspected these creatures, whatever they were, didn't have *less* venom than the smaller predators.

This time, at least, he heard Shill approaching. He turned to face the trapper, his hand openly on his quickshooter as the man emerged from the woods.

Teer was almost surprised that the man didn't have the furs from the bears already stripped and over his shoulder, but he saw the thoughtful look in the Zeeanan's eyes as he stepped up to the campfire.

"Ghost-bears," he said flatly. "You 'n your friend are lucky men. Know one bigger breed—but ghost magic and snow-bears don' come down here."

The name triggered a memory, a book *Teer* had read, not Abray. A book of children's stories, really, but it had contained a tale warning about the mysterious bears of the southern mountain ranges. Ghost-bears were supposed to be invisible and dangerous, but more spirit than monster, beings that could be spoken and even negotiated with.

Teer hadn't sensed much of *that* in the bears that had come at them the previous night. Just a hungry beast with dangerous natural abilities.

"Ghost-bears, huh," he said aloud. "Guess we are lucky. Could have been a lot worse."

"Should be dead," Shill said flatly. "But you live, bears don't. In trouble, though."

"We'll make it," Teer replied firmly. Once Kard was awake, he hoped the other man's healing magic would be able to finish what Teer's effort had started. Then they'd load Star up with all of their gear and walk her into town.

"Friend hurt bad," Shill observed. "Ghost-bear poison too. Need best healer. Good one in Cossax, Nerami." He paused. "Poison kill, never wake."

The man's odd speech didn't muffle his meaning, and Teer shivered, glancing back at the lean-to. Abray's concoction seemed to be helping, but he was truly relying on Kard waking up and being able to fix himself.

He gave Shill a level glare.

"We'll make it," he repeated. "Unless you've got a horse around you can lend us, we're stuck here anyway."

"Don't have horse," Shill conceded. "Have friends, though. Ghost-bear valuable. Fur, teeth, claws... Can't carry whole carcass."

Teer waited silently. He thought he saw the man's point, but he didn't want to raise his own hopes or commit to anything.

"If give the carcasses, walk to Cossax, get friends with wagon," Shill offered. "Must come back to get carcasses, get you and friend. Bring to Cossax in trade for bears?"

The ghost-bears were rare enough that Teer had only heard of them in a storybook. Their hides and other pieces were probably worth a lot more than a wagon ride—but Teer also wasn't going to do anything with the carcasses himself.

"Okay," he told the strange trapper. "The bears are yours if you can get us into town with our gear."

Shill eyed him for a dozen heartbeats or so, then nodded sharply. He scooped up his carrying frame—it took him a lot longer to put it on than it had to take off—and then set off toward the road at a steady lope.

It was only as the man vanished into the woods that Teer realized Shill had never even asked his name. Something about that didn't sit quite right... but if he could get Teer and Kard to a healer, Teer would handle being a bit uncomfortable.

———

TEER TOOK the time to pack up all of their gear. He'd removed Star's saddle once he'd found her, but he made sure that he had everything packed onto both of the saddles, except for the immediate supplies he was using to take care of Kard.

He wasn't wholly sure how to conceal Kard's ears and skin tone from strangers if they were being transported to town, until he realized that it was cold enough that the man's face and ears needed protection from frostbite.

Teer wrapped cloth around Kard's head, covering his long ears, and laid a protective mask over his face to guard it from the wind and chill. It would both conceal his face and protect him from the wind if they were moving.

The second dose of the antivenom draught was just as difficult to get into Kard as the first, but this time, he was certain the color on his friend's face was starting to recover. He swapped the bindings and the poultice over the gut wound, grimacing as he saw the state of the injury.

Even with the Kotan poultice, he needed to sew up the slash. At least what he could see confirmed the guts themselves had been pierced, which meant he *could* stitch it.

Boiling water, needle, thread. It wasn't a pleasant process, but Kard didn't wake up at any point. Teer was no seamstress, but his mother had been, and she'd made sure he had a passable hand with a needle— more for this exact purpose than for clothing, he knew.

Once the wound had been stitched, he put a new poultice and new bandages on it, wrapping them carefully around Kard's body before putting his friend back on his side.

He didn't expect Shill and his wagon to arrive until the morning, if he returned at all. That meant he could get some rest.

The few minutes of sleep next to the fire had been as helpful as they'd been unwise, but he needed more rest if he was going to be nursing Kard through this mess.

9

Teer was awake with the dawn, checking on his patient and the fire he'd put out before going to sleep. Kard was still breathing steadily, but his color was nowhere near normal and he still didn't seem to be waking up.

He finished the awkward process of giving an unconscious patient a liquid medicine and carefully laid him back down before he heard the sound of hooves and wheels.

The camp was far enough into the trees that even he hadn't heard anything from the road the previous day. Shill had almost certainly been moving through the woods to avoid being seen on the road himself when he'd spotted the campfire.

That thought fit into an uncomfortable pattern, and Teer made sure he had both of his quickshooters on him and loaded as he waited for the strangers to approach through the trees. Shill was after the ghost-bear carcasses, but that didn't mean he wasn't a threat.

He rose to meet them when he could see the group through the trees. His armored duster shifted around him as he unbuckled it to make sure he could reach his guns, then he waved to the strangers.

"That you, Shill?" he called out.

"With friends!" Shill replied. "Promised."

"So you did." Teer glanced over the other two men and the wagon. *Wagon* was probably a strong term for the vehicle, but a larger cart would have difficulty fitting through the trees. This one was small enough to be pulled by a single horse but had four wheels and looked sturdy enough to hold two bears and a few men.

"Howdy, stranger," the woman driving the wagon said cheerfully. She had similar faded brown coloring to Shill, though her sharper features and short-cropped black hair didn't suggest she was family to the trapper. The third was another Zeeanan man, probably larger than Shill and the driver put together, with a shaven scalp.

Both of Shill's friends were dressed much the same, in jeans of machine-woven cloth and decently fitted fur jackets. The clothes were practical and, while hardly fancy, of much higher quality than anything Shill was wearing.

"Shill said there were two ghost-bear carcasses out here, of all things," the driver continued. "Those are rare as snake milk, I'll say. Never even *seen* one, but I've heard of 'em."

"I hadn't," Teer said with a chuckle. "Not till they jumped us in the night." He gestured toward the carcasses. "Shill saw 'em; he knows where they are. You'll have space for my friend and our gear?"

"Sure," she agreed. "You'll have to walk with Shill and Koe, though. It's not that big a cart!"

Koe was presumably the big Zeeanan, who was the visibly armed member of the three with an unusual hunter with a wide barrel. The breechloader fired rounds at least twice the size Teer was used to, he figured.

Rounds for bears, he supposed.

"If you can take our gear, I'll stick on my horse and keep an eye out for trouble for all of us," Teer told her.

"That'll be handy," she said. She hadn't offered a name, though she had named the other two. A flick of the reins moved the cart in the direction of the carcasses and Teer watched her go.

Shill and Koe had dismounted, with the trapper leading the way. The big man seemed to be watching Teer rather than his apparent boss.

Teer met Koe's gaze. The stranger shrugged at him and then turned away.

Even without Abray's memories fueling extra paranoia, Teer hoped he would have realized the trio was planning to rob him.

————

TEER PACKED up everything into the saddles and saddlebags. He rigged a stretcher for lifting Kard into the wagon when they returned—whatever the three were planning, he was certain they were going to come back—and checked on his friend's vitals.

Still unconscious. He'd want to swap the bandages around noon, by which time he was still hoping to be in Cossax.

The sound of the locals returning told him that was going to be more difficult than he'd initially hoped. The wagon was much heavier, but there was a set of footsteps that was separated from the cart.

At a guess, Koe had split from the wagon to circle around behind.

The cart emerged from the trees again. Shill was walking alongside the vehicle, grinning from ear to ear as he kept looking at the two slumped forms in the wagon bed. Something in the demeanor of Shill's "friends" told Teer that Shill wasn't going to get a fair share of what the two carcasses were worth, but they would at least pay the man.

"I figure those are worth more than a ride to town," Teer said wryly as the wagon approached. "But a ride is what I need, and the furs are no use to me."

He glanced around.

"Where's Koe?" he asked. "I'll need a hand from someone getting my friend into the wagon."

"About that," the driver said, her voice still cheerful and friendly. "You know ghost-bears are poisonous, don't you? Your friend is dead; he just ain't realized it yet."

"Shill said there's a healer in Cossax who can help him. I owe him to try," Teer told her. He was listening carefully, tracking Koe's movements by sound. The man was sneaky, but Teer had trained his senses against Kotan scouts.

She looked down at him sadly.

"Thing is, Cossax is a poor town," she said. "And a glance at you tells me you ain't poor. All this gear for two men, and one of 'em dead? To my eyes, it just ain't fair. So, you're going to—"

Teer moved. He wasn't sure what he'd heard, but Koe's shot missed him by a yard or more.

His own shot hit Koe's gun. He hadn't been *intending* to—he probably *could* have made the shot like that, but he had half a second to draw, aim and fire, and had only been aiming for center mass.

The hunter fell from the Zeeanan's grip, and Teer knew that the driver also heard the big man's yelp of pain and surprise.

He had both his guns out, one trained on Koe and the other on the driver. Her hands had gone under the blanket over her legs, but she'd frozen at the sight of his quickshooter.

"You'll be takin' your hands out slow now, won't you?" Teer told her. "And Koe? I think you should come closer. It's goin' to give me a headache, keepin' an eye on both of you at once, and I'd hate to have to shoot one of you just to spare me that."

I will kill with only need.

The memory of the oath Abray had sworn rang in his head—the same one the ghost in his head suggested he should honor, if not exactly swear himself.

Koe slowly stepped out of the trees, his hands spread wide. He held the hunter in one of them, but its lever was locked back, marking the chamber as empty.

Plus, the damage from his shot was equally visible, and Teer wouldn't have wanted to fire the gun without a lot of repairs.

"Look," he told the woman. "By the Courts and the Nightmare Sea, what is your *name*?"

There was a long silence, long enough for Koe to join the other two where Teer could cover them all without stretching his eyes or his arms.

"Soiell," she finally answered. The false friendliness was gone now.

Her tone was level, two syllables barely enough to hear any quiver from her staring down a gun.

"Soiell," he repeated. "My name is Teer. I am a licensed Unity Hunter: my job is to bring criminals in for justice. Would I find a bounty with your face on it if I dragged you to the Wardkeeper?"

She sniffed, either in disdain or against a suddenly cold gust of wind.

"No," she told him. "This ain't the west *or* the east. In the mountains, you do what you gotta do."

"To a lot of folk, what I should do is shoot you all dead," Teer pointed out. "If you pull the gun under that blanket on me, I will. You understand me, Soiell?"

She looked at him curiously for a heartbeat, then nodded.

"I understand you, Hunter Teer," she said. "And the meaning that you're not going to shoot us?"

"I need a ride to Cossax for me and my friend," he reminded her. "I don't care about those furs or claws or whatever you're goin' to pull from the ghost-bears.

"The deal was transport in exchange for the bears. I'm fine with that deal. We keep that deal, no one gets hurt. Get me to Nerami while my friend lives… Assuming they *exist*, that is?"

He spared a sharp glance at Shill. He still had both guns out, though he'd relaxed his grip slightly, enough that Koe and Soiell would realize he didn't have the weapons pointed directly at them anymore.

"She exists," Soiell confirmed. There was another long silence.

"Shill, Koe, let's get our friend Teer's gear and friend loaded onto the cart," she told the two men, the cheer back in her voice. "We've got a deal to keep, after all!"

oe helped Teer bring Kard into the house, a two-story building just off Cossax's main street—which was also the military road through the Latch Mountains, and so in better repair than what he saw of the rest of the town's streets.

Shill and Soiell, to his surprise, brought in the two saddles with their saddlebags and equipment. Once Kard was in a bed, he met the three at the door.

"I'm hopin' those ghost-bear hides are worth it to you," he told them. "But I appreciate your help."

"Mare is at hitching post to left," Shill replied.

"No one steals in this town," Soiell assured him. "We do that on the highway."

It was both a joke and an admission that they *had* tried to rob him. And, well, kill him. Koe had *not* been aiming to scare.

"Then I hope I don't meet anyone from here on the highway," he replied lightly, though he knew Soiell would catch the warning. She struck him as the type to hear it as a warning even if he *didn't* mean one.

"I think you'll be fine," Soiell said with a chuckle and a wave. "Six inns in town. Ask Nerami for one, since if I gave you one, you'd go to any other."

She wasn't wrong, and Teer gave her a deep nod. For all that they'd tried to kill him and it had been an awkwardly silent ride into Cossax, the trio had kept their word—and there'd never been the slightest hint of second-guessing after the first attempt.

"Good luck, you three," he told them. Far away from him, preferably, but still.

"Same to you, Hunter Teer," Soiell replied. With the same silent addition, he was quite sure, as the three exited the doctor's house with haste.

"So, now the show-and-tell is over, would you care to tell me what I am dealing with?" the healer, who had done nothing so far but direct them to a bed for Kard. "My prices are not cheap, either, so I hope you have the stones for this."

Teer turned to examine his best hope for Kard's life. She was an older Merik woman with gray-streaked waist-length braids who spoke with a precise accent it took him a moment to place. She sounded like Kard had when he'd worn his true face and used his birth name to get Teer out of prison.

She was from the west, the coast—and the *cities* of the west, where the Unity's true power lay. And where the reality that all of the Unity were Spehari slaves was closer to the surface than others, he suspected.

"I can afford your prices," Teer told her confidently. "And, I hope, your silence."

Nerami was quiet for a moment, studying him in turn. Her gaze was meticulous, sweeping him from head to toe in a manner that was completely clinical and a touch unsettling.

"Merik. Hunter. Armed and armored, and that duster has seen more than just weather," she observed. "Patient is of a similar build, so I'm presuming his duster is among that pile of junk your friends dropped in my front hall."

"You are correct," Teer agreed. "But there are secrets a dying man cannot keep from his doctor, and they are secrets that must be kept.

The price of a life and your silence, Doctor? He has been poisoned by ghost-bear talons."

She inhaled sharply through suddenly visible perfect teeth.

"That will require some interesting medicines and time," she told him. "If it has been too long since the infection, even I may not be able to save him. I must examine him... if you can pay. For the work and silence, five stones."

Teer held her gaze as he reached into his duster. The inside pocket acted as a sealed purse, but the redcrystal stones were easily distinguishable from the glass shards by touch. He withdrew eight stones and held them out to her.

"Your silence may prove more expensive than you expect," he murmured. "I recognize its value."

There were Inquisitors hunting Kard, the most feared of the Unity's enforcers. They could force the truth from the Merik healer, but if she kept her mouth shut, they'd never know to ask.

She glanced down at the stones and raised an eyebrow.

"Take a seat; put the stones on the desk," she ordered, waving toward the furniture in question.

Teer did as instructed. The main floor of the house had few internal walls that he could see—he guessed that the kitchen was behind the ones he could see and that Nerami lived on the second floor.

The open space remaining was divided into two clear sections. One had a trio of beds and moving screens to provide privacy. The other had a handful of chairs, a full wall of bookshelves, waist-high cabinets Teer guessed held records of some kind, and a desk that incorporated more cabinets.

All of the furniture had a familiar shape, if not color. It had been assembled from standard planks from a sawmill like the one in Alvid. The trees that had gone into the mill hadn't been the fast-growing but sturdy trees of the eastern plains. These were darker and looked heavier to his eye, but the lengths and widths of the planks were the same.

He pulled the seat around so he could both see Nerami work and watch the door. She hadn't asked him to leave his guns anywhere, and he wouldn't have anyway.

She removed the wrap around Kard's head just as Teer took his seat and she gasped. Teer caught a sharp glance back at him, but to her credit, she kept her focus on her patient.

Step by step and piece by piece, she quickly but gently undressed the El-Spehari. Teer guessed she was doing a visual inventory as she did so, but she said nothing to him.

Finally, she came to the gut wound. There was a hint of relief in her body language as she carefully touched the bandages, not immediately removing them, and then she stepped back and turned to Teer.

"How long ago was this?" she asked.

"A candlemark or two after nightfall, two nights ago," he replied. "Some candlemarks less than three days."

"Are you certain?" Nerami demanded, her tone suddenly sharp. "I will have to check a source, but I understand ghost-bear venom to generally be lethal within four days. I would expect a far greater progression of discoloration and greater difficulty breathing than the patient is showing.

"Spehari reaction to venoms is not a subject I have treatises on, of course, but I wouldn't expect it to be that different."

Honesty seemed like the best way to make sure Kard lived through the venom, so Teer pulled the canteen with its last dose of antivenom draught from inside his duster, putting it on the desk carefully.

"The initial reactions seemed to mirror wolfen venom," he told her. "I knew a recipe for an antivenom that handled that with some rough side effects."

Worse in women, he realized, as the memory of an uncomfortable conversation between Abray and Opal, after she'd moved in with him, about the fact that the antivenom was the more likely source of her barrenness than the wolfen poison itself.

Nerami grabbed the canteen, opened it and took a sniff.

"Odala's Fourth Draught," she identified it. "An extremely effective antivenom against almost any toxin. It is difficult to find ingredients for and inflicts nontrivial internal damage itself. Of course, the harder-to-find ingredients are native to this area, aren't they?"

"I had most in our medical kit," Teer confirmed. "Blue nettlebrush root was difficult with the snow, but at least it was root and not flowers. Moonglow petals were harder, since only a few of the plants have any blooms left in early winter."

"An herbalist, I see," Nerami said. "Of course, there are *better* solutions for treating wolfen or ghost-bear venom, but Odala's Fourth is old and reliable. Especially if the patient will die without intervention."

Teer didn't exactly have a solid list of herbal recipes. Half of Abray's herbal repertoire had been assembled by a level of experimentation that would have been suicidal for someone without Adept self-healing. The other half was from his training as an Adept—and *Teer* wasn't entirely certain which half was which yet.

"I knew it wasn't safe, but he was dying," Teer murmured. "And he hasn't woken up, which would have prevented him using his power to heal himself. Can you save him?"

"If you had brought him to me the morning after the injury, without question," Nerami told him bluntly. "If you had brought him to me now, three days later, *without* giving him the antivenom, he would be doomed.

"Now, while the venom remains the largest problem, the draught has done additional damage that we must watch, and three days of unconsciousness has its own risks."

She shook her head.

"I am *very* good, Hunter Teer," she told him. "I believe I can fix this, but it will take time. I must change his bindings, assess the intestinal wound—and how much damage the draught did to the intestines as well. His bowels do not appear to have been breached, but the draught could cause enough internal damage to turn a scrape into a fissure."

Teer shivered as he realized that his care—while the only thing that had kept Kard alive—had also carried a risk of making things even worse.

"Can I help?" he asked.

"No." She shook her head. "What you can do for me, young man, is go to the guest room upstairs and sleep for a few candlemarks. I don't care how much money you have; I don't need a second patient while I'm dealing with this gentleman!"

"His presence here needs to be quiet, though his race far more so," Teer warned. "I can stand gua—"

"Hunter Teer, my son is this town's Wardkeeper," Nerami said acidly. "My daughters run the general store and the largest inn. The younger's husband is a barber, generally considered the middle of the three in town. The elder's wife runs the workshop.

"If you need something in this town, my kids can get it for you. And if someone decided to make my life difficult, they wouldn't find anything they needed in Cossax!"

She gave him a reproving look.

"Go sleep, young man," she repeated. "And let me get to work on your friend. I promise you: he is in the best hands you were going to find in these mountains."

———

THE GUEST ROOM had a sign on the door and was unlocked, unlike the rest of the doors upstairs. It had the same bed as the clinic on the ground floor and one of the same chairs. There was no other furniture in the space, though a hand-knit rug had been hung on the wall with care.

It wasn't until Teer woke up—having fallen into the bed fully clothed—that he recognized the rug. It had been in his not-dream about Abray, and he remembered it vividly from the other man's memories.

Age had worn down the colors of Opal's work. There were clear signs where it had been repaired—by, Teer suspected, a better weaver than Opal—but the pattern had been preserved and it had ended up as a piece of wall art.

That raised many questions, but his body raised a more important one. Nerami, for her part, looked up from examining Kard and pointed to a backdoor from the house wordlessly when he came down the stairs.

The outhouse was easy enough to find, and he returned to the house. There was a sink by the back door with soap, and he took that as a hint about the cleanliness expected in a doctor's workspace.

He washed his hands, forearms and face carefully before crossing to the bed where Kard still lay. His companion didn't look any worse, but the discoloration seemed to have settled in across his skin.

"This venom is a cruel beast," Nerami told him. "I have done what I can for now. I've cleaned and redressed the wound and given him a more tailored antivenom. Ghost-bears are rare here, but they're common enough in the south. Shiggan mountaineers have stories about the monsters, and their healers have traditions about what to do for a wounded hunter who stumbles down from the hills, turning purple."

"How is he?" Teer asked quietly.

"Thanks to your draught, I think he is going to live," the doctor said. That was the most confident she'd been so far, which he took as a good sign. "He was lucky in how shallow the blow was and again in how his body has chosen to handle the draught.

"Were he Arani, I would warn that he would have trouble breathing for the rest of his life," Nerami continued grimly. "No worse than those who smoke various herbs, and a fair price for a life. Since he is Spehari, I believe he will be able to fix the damage to his lungs once he recovers.

"Spehari healing magic is as poorly studied as their physiology." She snorted. "Or, at least, the studies are not available to Arani students. I doubt their healers have no treatises or training."

"As do I," Teer agreed. He looked down at Kard. Even with the color marks of the venom, Kard was still paler than either of the Merik in the room, though Teer knew he wasn't as pale as a true-blood Spehari.

"Odd to see a man go so far to save a Spehari," she said quietly. "Or to see a Spehari in Hunter's gear, for that matter."

He glanced over at her, and she gave him a look that he suspected she'd mastered over being the mother of three children grown to adulthood. Even his mother wasn't that good at it.

"I promise *silence*, not *no questions*, Teer."

He sighed, shucking his coat off and pulling down the side of his shirt collar to show the magical brand where his neck met his shoulder.

"I am Bound to him," he told her simply. "Bondsman, bondservant, Bound, however you want to classify it, I am magically linked to him. I know when he's awake; I know when he's sleeping, how he's feeling."

All he'd really picked up through the bond the last few days was that Kard was asleep, which told him some of the limits of the magic.

"While I understand that I will *survive* his death, I have no real interest in testing that theory," he continued drily. "I owe him my life, and we have been friends and companions for over a turning. I'd have done as much for a friend of any race, so long as I had the money."

Teer didn't have the amount of paper wealth Kard apparently had tucked away in various places across the Unity, but Kard had covered most of their working expenses from his larger share of the bounties they'd actually taken. Only one of which hadn't been callipsuses, he realized.

He hadn't really thought of that. The first bounty he'd ever done had been unquestionably black-and-white, hunting down a murderer and his gang. The *second* had been Lora, who they'd smuggled to safety.

They had earned more money delivering callipsus heads to Captain-Magistrate Taran than they had delivering regular bounties, but it was the latter that Teer still thought of as defining him.

It was about protecting people, whatever label they put on it.

"I have known many Spehari in my turnings," Nerami finally said. "Not many would go out of their way to save the life of any Arani, even one useful to them. But then, I suppose I've never met one working as a Hunter, either."

"Your silence is appreciated," Teer told her. He wasn't going to tell her that Kard was a half-blood, but even *a Spehari who was a Hunter* could lead the wrong people after them. "I can—"

"If you were going to offer me more money to keep my peace, young man, you have much to learn about understanding people," she cut him off. "Your friend is resting as easily as he's going to for a while now.

"I have not told my son what is going on, but he is a clever lad, and I didn't let him in while you were sleeping," she continued. "There has been a Wardwatch reading a broadsheet across the road for a full candlemark now. The clinic is being watched for my safety. Your friend will *also* be safe."

Teer nodded silently. He wasn't sure how far he could trust Nerami's integrity, not after Shill, but he had little choice.

"Now, I will be blunt. I appreciate you washing up when you came in, but you stink of the road," she told him. "Your horse needs a proper stable and you need a proper bath. My daughter, Levina, has her inn a hundred yards down the way, next door to Loua's, the big workshop her wife runs.

"The 'shop can help with anything you need for gear or for your horse, and Levina's people can stable your horse, feed you and find you a tub of water to throw yourself in."

He glanced back at Kard.

"I promise you, Teer, my patient is safer here than anywhere else he could be," she assured him. "Your horse has been tied up to a hitching post for several candlemarks, and you haven't bathed in at least a tenday.

"You can use the guest room again tonight and leave your things here. Just… take some clothes with you for Levina's people to launder while you wash."

There was an expression of long-standing patience and experience on her face as she smiled at him.

"I know men like you, Teer. You've got maybe one clean outfit left in those saddlebags. Your friend will be fine—and might be happier when he wakes if you get *his* clothes cleaned, too!"

11

The Cossax Inn and Stable was clearly older than much of the town around it. It was, in fact, old enough that Teer recognized it from Abray's memories.

Well, part of it. The central common room around the bar and kitchen had already existed all those turnings ago, though the wing of rooms to the south of it had clearly been demolished and replaced with a sturdier structure of brick and stone. The core common room had been reinforced as well, but the building was recognizably the same inn that Cossax had been born around.

Loua's Workshop, right next door, was less recognizable except for one thing: the sign hanging above the courtyard entrance. He remembered Abray's wife and the two women laughing as they'd drafted the design in Abray's kitchen.

The only text was Loua's name, with an artistic rendering of a Zeeanan woman in a red dress holding a chisel in one hand and a hammer in the other—with the handle of an unclear third tool emerging from her cleavage in a rather suggestive manner.

Like the rug in Nerami's guest room, it had clearly been fixed and updated, with new paint to pick out older colors as they faded, but the sign still hung proudly on the main street. The workshop it labeled was far larger than the cramped shed Loua had worked out of when she'd done everything from tool repair to stonemasonry for a village of two hundred souls, but the continuity was there.

It was a strangely warming feeling to realize that not only had Abray actually existed, people he remembered had built things that lasted. Businesses and buildings and dreams.

A young Merik woman at the inn's front desk greeted him cheerily as he stepped in.

"Welcome, welcome! How can we help you in Cossax today, sir?"

Despite his nap at Nerami's, he found himself a bit taken aback by the enthusiasm. It didn't help that he could hear at least two-thirds of the conversations in the building as a background rumble, though without focusing, he couldn't make out details.

From Abray's memories, his perception that his senses were getting sharper over time was entirely correct. It would slow down eventually, according to what the Orders had understood, but there would be a period of a few turnings right after his powers awoke where his hearing and sight would get noticeably sharper over time.

After that, his senses would continue to improve, but it wouldn't be quite as noticeable as it was right then, where every time he entered a town, it was a step closer to utter chaos.

"Sorry," he said, shaking his head. "I'm watching a patient of Nerami's, and she told me to come here to arrange stabling for my horse—and, well, laundry and a bath."

She smiled widely at him.

"Of course. Your name?"

"I'm Teer. You?" he asked her without thinking.

"I'm Rys." The smile was somehow wider and more brilliant. "Your horse is outside?"

"Yes, dark brown mare named Star," he said. "I have a couple of bags of laundry for myself and a friend, if I can get those handled?"

"We can do all of that here at the Cossax Inn," she assured him, the practiced measure of her promise thrown off slightly by the wink she gave him. "I'll have the cousins take care of your horse if you'll show her to me. I'll grab your laundry and show you to the bath."

"Of course, there is the matter of payment..."

———

A FEW MINUTES LATER—AND the discovery that "the cousins" was a collection of teenage Merik girls ranging from thirteen to sixteen turnings, all of whom were definitely related to Loua and Marie—Teer was comfortable in the certainty that Star was going to be taken care of.

Or, perhaps more accurately, spoiled to within an inch of her hardworking life. The teenage girls were clustered around her head, cooing over her, when he passed the saddlebags of laundry to Rys with a moment of embarrassment.

She hung around long enough to take the clothes he'd been wearing—through the door, thankfully—then left him to the bath, which was worth every one of the shards he'd paid for it.

Hot water. Soap. A bathtub long enough and deep enough for even someone of Teer's size to fully immerse himself. It was luxury—and bath, laundry and five days prepaid stabling had set him back twenty shards, so he was *paying* for that luxury.

Eventually, the water cooled enough to no longer be quite as luxurious. He scrubbed off and dressed in his last clean jeans and shirt. The jeans were undyed denim, cut and sewn from machine-woven cloth by his mother. The shirt was one of several black ones he'd picked up from a tailor under Doka's guidance after they'd brought in his first bounty.

The shirt was still open when Rys opened the door to check in on him. She got an eyeful of his naked chest, and from the way she didn't look away, that had been at least part of the point of coming in without knocking.

"Yes?" he finally asked after an awkward moment.

"I wanted to check if you need anything, Mr. Teer, sir," she said all in one breath. "The bath was fine?"

Teer swallowed an amused shake of his head. Young as Rys felt to him, he realized she was actually *older* than him—and the feeling of youthfulness he was getting from her had nothing to do with Abray's memories.

"The bath was incredible," he told her honestly, buttoning up his shirt. "I trust 'the cousins' have Star settled in the stable?"

"Settled, brushed, fed and probably petted more than she's been in the last turning," Rys said with a grin of amusement. "She's a very sweet horse; I checked in on her myself to be sure."

"I appreciate it." Rys had almost certainly contributed to the petting, though Teer wasn't going to take the bet on how much Star had been petted in the last turning.

She was a very good horse and took good care of him.

"Your laundry will be ready in the morning," the girl continued. "Is there anything else I—we—can do for you this afternoon?"

Teer caught her slip of the tongue and bit down on his own amusement. Rys was gorgeous, but she didn't know anything about *him* except that she liked the look of his body. Some days, that might be enough for him, but not with Kard unconscious.

"I need to get back to Nerami's and my friend," he said. "I'll be by in the morning to pick up the clothes and check in on Star. She and I both get nervous if we don't see each other!"

12

Teer woke up and took a few heartbeats to place himself. He didn't sleep in a bed often anymore, even one as simple as the guest-room bed. Once he'd placed himself, he tried to work out what had woken him up—and then he caught it.

Kard was awake.

He was downstairs in a breath, probably pushing the limits of how fast he should move around strangers, but he didn't want Kard to wake up uncertain and unaware of where he was.

Stepping past the screens up to his friend's bed, it didn't *look* like Kard was awake. There was a bell at the side of the bed, set up so that if the bed moved significantly, it would ring to let Nerami know her patient was awake.

"I'm here," Teer told Kard.

There was a silence, but he knew the other man was awake. Slowly, Kard opened his eyes without moving, then turned his head slightly to find Teer.

"I feel like shit," he whispered. "Where *is* 'here'?"

"Doctor's office in Cossax," Teer said. "Brought you in wrapped against frostbite, so she's the only one who knows you're Spehari. I paid her for her silence, and I think she can be trusted."

79

So far as Teer could tell, Nerami had married into the descendants of Abray's friends. Nothing in the old Adept's memories told him that pair was anything less than trustworthy, and the probably great-great-grandchildren he'd met at the inn had lived up to that expectation.

Kard exhaled.

"In town? How long was I out?"

"Five days," Teer said quietly. Two in the wilderness, then three more in Nerami's care. "The beasts that ambushed us in the forest had venom on their claws along with their magic. You were nearly gutted, and you *were* poisoned.

"I had a recipe for an antivenom in my head that kept you breathing until we got to town. Nerami is the healer; she's worked miracles, I think, to keep you alive."

Kard nodded slightly, glanced at the bell attached to the bed and then consciously moved enough to set it off. With Teer's extra-sensitive hearing, he appreciated the silent warning.

Nerami came down the steps a lot more slowly than Teer had.

"He's awake, Nerami," Teer called softly as she reached the bottom of the steps. "Seems coherent, too."

"That's good." The gray-haired doctor stepped through the screens and gave Kard a visual once-over. "My Lord, welcome back to the world of the living. You've had a difficult few days."

"I gather. And I gather I owe you my life, Nerami, and that is not a debt I admit lightly," he told her. "Not least, I am not a *lord*. Just Kard."

"Your friend is paying the bill, Kard," Nerami replied. "That was the only debt you owed. I am a professional, and I take pride in my skills.

"Now, I need to examine you, and I would prefer you not use healing magic until I have completed that exam. If nothing else, I believe I can allow you to apply said magic more effectively, and you will be quite weak for a while yet."

———

Teer made himself scarce by going over to the Cossax Inn to collect food. The healer had sent him over more than once before, so he'd learned she had a standing order with the hotel's kitchen for her own meals.

She also had an account there, which he'd refused to let them put the meals he grabbed on. If she'd ordered in every meal for the three days she'd been treating Kard, it would have cost him less than thirty shards. Expensive for hotel meals but not badly so.

A blue shard, the smallest official currency of the Unity, was generally considered good for a traveler's meal and drink. Cossax Hotel's meals ranged from two to five shards—the most expensive costing as much as a night in their smaller rooms—and Nerami's preferences were to the simpler end of their fare.

So were Teer's, if he was honest, and the breakfast he brought back to Nerami's house was simply three of the same plate: a collection of eggs, toast, and fried ham.

He laid them out on the desk, listening through the screens to the litany of remaining issues that Nerami was telling Kard. She probably thought she was speaking quietly enough he couldn't hear her.

"The cut across your stomach is healing rapidly. Your young Teer did a good job of stitching you up, and he was using an anti-infection poultice that I would love the recipe for," she said crisply. "The venom got into all of your blood, however, and there may be long-term consequences for that. There is damage throughout your body. Almost every muscle you have will have some level of stiffness. Most should fade quickly, but some will be more stubborn, and I can't predict which ones.

"You were unconscious for five days. That will also cause issues with your muscles. I did my best to keep you hydrated and provide essentials, but I imagine you are very hungry. You must eat carefully— and I would strongly recommend against using magic until you do so."

"Is that a topic you learned about in the west, doctor?" Kard asked quietly.

"You know that is a banned topic for non-Spehari doctor-trainees," Nerami replied. "I am making presumptions on basic principles of how the body functions. While I have not examined a Spehari before, your flesh and muscles and blood appear to work the same way as an Arani."

"Indeed. You are correct, so far as I know," he told her. "I was curious if you had received… illicit training. There are certainly some, though they are usually Bonded or Marked."

Teer heard Nerami shiver.

"I have never been willing to let a Spehari own me that directly, Lord Kard."

Kard didn't challenge her use of the title that time, Teer noticed. He had finished organizing the breakfasts on the table and was about to go get them when Nerami spoke again.

"There is one other thing," she told Kard. "Your Teer knew an old —and quite dangerous, frankly—recipe for antivenom that I had only encountered once or twice in my training. Odala's Fourth Draught hasn't been actively used in sixty turnings, at least, and I only recognized the smell because one of my mentors was working on a full investigation of Odala's work.

"In this case, when you were going to die, it was a correct response, but there can be severe long-term consequences from it." She paused. "First off, you have a set of quite nasty internal burns, mostly down your esophagus and into your lungs, but they're also an aggravating factor in your gut health.

"Those *should* react to your healing magic as well as anything else, but I wanted to make sure you knew the injuries were there to heal."

"I had guessed something from how hard breathing is," Kard said. "A fair trade for *still* breathing, in my opinion."

"I am not sure you will feel the same about the rest," Nerami told him grimly. "I am aware of… the fertility concerns of the Spehari, Kard. The main reason that a doctor wouldn't use Odala's Fourth Draught now, even beyond its difficult-to-acquire ingredients, is because any regime of multiple doses has a high probability of causing sterility.

"Given the general limited fertility of Spehari, I have to presume that the use of the draught has rendered you completely sterile."

There was a grim warning to her tone but also an undercurrent of fear. If Kard were truly Spehari, Teer suspected that would be devastating news—news that could easily drive a wedge between a master and a loyal retainer.

Except that Teer knew that Kard was *El-Spehari*, and part of the reason the Unity had been happy to raise and train the half-bloods as enforcers was that they were *already* sterile. Kard could never have had children no matter what.

"Thank you for being honest with me," Kard said levelly. "That is… disconcerting, but I still feel that it was a price I am prepared to accept, given that I *am* still breathing. You do not need to worry about Teer, Doctor. I value his life as much as my own."

Teer felt a flush of warmth run through him and gave himself a moment to settle before heading out to tell them their food was ready.

13

Despite Nerami's warnings, they set out a day later—when Teer's hearing picked up a dragon coming into the town.

Teer wasn't sure what he'd expected from the dragon dock. It was on the north side of the town, and at first, he didn't even realize there was anything there. A warehouse stood between it and the rest of the town, and that was all he saw.

Kard knew what he was looking for and led the way, with Star trailing behind them on a lead. To anyone except Teer, he probably looked perfectly fine—not least because he had his illusion back up, wrapping him in the visage of a Merik man who looked like Teer's cousin.

Anyone who knew the pair might suspect that the man with Teer was Kard, but hopefully he looked different enough to be unrecognizable from any posters or images that were being passed out.

"They'll stop there," Kard told him, gesturing toward a narrow pole that Teer hadn't even noticed. It stood about a dozen feet tall, about thirty feet past the end of the warehouse.

From the pole, Teer found the dragon line. Two parallel tracks of iron, darkened with ash and dirt rather than whatever process had blackened the blade slung across his back.

They came down from the mountains in the west and rose up again as they headed east. The warehouse and the wooden pole were the only markers near the line, which was enough to let Teer trace its route through the town.

Cossax was shaped by the dragon line, he saw. There wasn't much to the valley the town sat in to the north of the line, but there was *nothing* of the town there. Every building, even the pens for sheep and cows and chickens, was on the south side of the dragon line. Except for the warehouse at the dock, in fact, there were no buildings north of an invisible boundary Teer judged to be thirty feet south of the line.

"I expected the dragon to be here already," Teer murmured. He could still hear the engine heading their way, a hissing and rumbling sound interspersed with occasional screams.

Even without *seeing* the thing, he could understand why it was called a dragon.

"The sounds can carry a surprisingly long way in mountains like this," Kard replied. "And the whistle is supposed to carry far enough to warn people it's coming. The Spehari might not care if your cart is on the dragon line for *your* sake, but they don't want to have to stop the dragon for repairs or cleanup."

Teer shivered at the cold bitterness in Kard's voice.

"The dragons must run on time. Not that the Unity tells civilians what the schedule *is*."

He nodded and looked to the west. Following the line, he spotted the dragon. It was still far enough away to be little more than a dark spot along the dragon line—or, he realized, a *series* of dark spots that stretched up the mountain behind it.

"Hey, Teer."

He turned to see Rys standing behind them. She was wearing a sturdy dress and cloak, far less form-fitting than the clothes she'd worn inside the hotel. Her hood was up, shrouding her face, and over-all, she looked like she was trying to hide.

He'd heard her approaching, but there were enough people moving around town that he wouldn't have registered her as a threat unless he heard a weapon—or she'd approached another half-dozen feet.

"Hi, Rys. Did I forget something at the inn?" he asked lightly, though he could tell it wasn't that. It also wasn't whatever spark of attraction she'd felt toward him in the hotel. This was serious, and that worried *him*.

"Mom sent me out to give you a warning word," she told him. "Your friend there is older, he's probably safe, but press squads have come through town every so often of late—and they're often on the dragons.

"Anyone of seventeen to thirty turnings without a clear job or apprenticeship is subject to call-up at the recruiter's discretion," Rys continued, in a tone that made it clear she was repeating someone else's words. "They grabbed one of the cousins without even *asking*, and he was working at the workshop.

"Mom said to tell you to keep your head down," she concluded. "I'm going to do just that, official job at the hotel and all. Be careful."

"Thank you," Teer told her. "We're going to be paying for passage, so that should help keep eyes off—and we're Unity-licensed."

"Might be safe. Might get hauled off to a rotting swamp to fight a lizard death goddess. Walk your path. May the Mountin' Stars watch you."

"And you, Rys. Be safe."

She disappeared back into the streets, lost in a mist that was rolling in only slightly faster than the dragon. The hanging cloud was beginning to shroud everything, and the sight sent a shiver down Teer's spine.

"Let me talk to the people on the dragon," Kard told him. "You handled everything well when those bears took me out, but this is more dangerous than you might think. In normal times, our licenses and coin would be enough to handle any suspicion, but if they're actively press-ganging youth for the Army..."

"I look like a prime soldier," Teer concluded into the silence, reaching over to stroke Star's mane, as much to reassure himself as the horse.

"Yes. And while *death goddess* is as shitty a description of the Kott religion as *rotting swamp* is of the northern wetlands, you still don't want to be sent to war against the Kott," his friend concluded.

Kard had, after all, fought on the same side as the Kott in the Sunset Rebellion. He knew how the lizards of the north made war. That didn't make Teer feel any happier about the sound of the press squads working through the towns.

The sound of the dragon beginning to slow down interrupted that thought, a sharp squeal of metal on metal. Teer looked back up at the closing machine and shivered.

It was painted red, with black streaks that might have been paint or might have been ash. A maw-like vent topped the dragon, fire visible in the red-black smoke belching from it. Light gleamed from what might have been eyes—or windows in a cabin that made Teer think of a great beast's head.

Behind the dragon came its cargo, a line of wagons linked together and fitted to the tracks of the dragon line. Dozens, maybe over a hundred, of the carts followed in the dragon's wake, pulled by its alchemical might.

The squeal of metal increased as the dragon approached the warehouse and stop marker. It rose to a crescendo that Teer thought would have hurt *anyone's* ears, let alone his, and then stopped with one last belch of fiery smoke.

The wagon immediately behind the dragon opened right away and a dozen soldiers in dark gray uniforms jumped out. Half of them moved up to take up watch positions around the dragon itself, while the others spread out to sweep the length of the dragon's tail.

More people followed from that wagon and the one behind it, plus a pair of men in white-and-gray uniforms. They saw Teer and Kard waiting and looked past them. One set off for the warehouse, gesturing for soldiers and workers to fall in behind him.

"Just wait," Kard muttered.

Finally, the second uniformed man stepped up to them.

"We're here for cargo drop. Tell the Wardkeeper we won't be stopping on our way back. Orders."

"Don't work for the Wardkeeper," Kard replied. "We're Hunters, followed a bounty this far west. Caught 'im, got paid—but we need to get back to work. Do you have space for two men and a horse to ride to Shiaray? We'll pay our way, standard rates."

The dragon-man snorted. He looked them up and down, taking in the gray dusters and the weapons, then snorted again.

"We're running mostly empty, if I'm honest," he admitted. "Orders. Need to see your papers—especially the boy's. There's some as are hiding from the draft, like they don't 'preciate Unity at all."

Kard held his hand out to Teer. Even without asking, Teer knew to take out his Hunter's papers—signed and sealed by Wardkeeper Ashan out of Carlon, a major wardtown along a river, well away from the dragon lines.

They were, from what he understood, more real than *Kard's*. His were signed to his real name, after all.

The dragon-man took both sets of papers and spent far too long reading them. He read faster than Teer could, but he was clearly reading for specific things.

"Fair enough, Hunters," he finally said. "There's a recruiting officer aboard with the troops; he'll want to be sure too. Figured we'd deal with any issues first."

"We are who we are, Dragonmaster," Kard said politely. "Standard rate for the passage?"

"Aye. From here to Shiaray, four days. No food, though the Unity quartermaster might sell you something. Twenty-five shards each for the pair of you, another fifty for the horse."

"We've food of our own; we're used to the road," the El-Spehari confirmed, pulling coins from his purse.

The total was a full stone—enough for both of them to have stayed in Cossax Hotel for a tenday—but Kard pulled out a handful of glass coins to pay it instead of a single redcrystal stone.

"Done and done. I'm Dragonmaster Gerg. Stable wagon is twenty-six; use the passenger wagon next to it." Gerg snorted. "There's nobody else in it, but don't make a mess. If there's a problem, the recruiter's got thirty solid men with him, plus our dragon-guard. I *will* make it your problem; hear me?"

"We hear you," Kard agreed. He waved for Teer to follow him and set off down the length of the dragon.

———

THE WAGONS WERE ALL NUMBERED. It had been done with chalk on slate panels, so it had been partially worn away on most of them, but enough remained to make the sequence clear. Twenty-six looked roughly like what Teer had expected, as much as he expected anything: it was a wooden stable on a solid platform with wheels beneath it.

The wheels were locked on to the dragon-line tracks, keeping the stable wagon with everyone else, and there was a ramp that the soldier with them showed them how to pull out. Teer led Star up into the wagon, then when he turned to thank their guide, the woman was already a dozen yards away, heading back to the group offloading from the front wagons.

"I feel like someone was expecting us to be unimpressed," Kard told him with a chuckle. "I have ridden like this before—and done it on dragons with longer tails and a *lot* more people."

Teer stepped off the ramp and into the stable, grimacing at the single open box. If there was one thing the ranch where he'd grown up had plenty of, it was *space*. Out in the east, he was used to stables that held stalls ranging from ten to fifteen feet square for individual horses.

The stable wagon was barely ten feet wide and only about thirty-five long. There was no division into individual stalls, though there was a bar along one side with clear spots for hitch ropes and feedbags.

There was some hay on the floor but not nearly enough, in Teer's opinion, and the crowding would be horrific if it actually held the dozen horses there were hitching points for.

Star would have it to herself, though, which was better. He hitched her to one of the points and pulled her cargo off. He heard her whinny in some relief and gave her a quick pet of apology—they'd loaded both her and poor Clack's saddle and supplies onto her, though they had walked her and he suspected she'd been more concerned about the precariousness of the arrangement than the weight.

"Just a few moments, girl," he assured her and set off to gather what hay there was. Combined with the supplies in the saddles, he thought he could make the space comfortable for her.

He couldn't imagine how the horses normally transported in the wagon handled it!

———

HAVING SETTLED Star down as best as he could, Teer saw that Kard had pulled the ramp up for him. There was a door at each end of the stable wagon, opening to a concerning connection to the next wagon.

The stable wagon's door was right up to the end of the wagon, leaving a two-foot drop to the ground. With the dragon not yet in motion, it was fine, but Teer could envisage the ground whipping away beneath him.

Several thick bars and hooks connected the stable to the passenger wagon ahead of it, which at least had a small balcony at the back to step onto. The gap wasn't even long enough to require a jump, but the thought of making it while the dragon moved didn't help Teer's comfort with the process.

He stepped over and entered the wagon ahead, which was only slightly less depressing than the stable wagon. The main cabin was a bit smaller than the stable, probably due to the balconies for getting onto and off the wagon.

There were ten rows of uncomfortable-looking benches, divided down the middle by a pathway that wasn't quite broad enough for Teer to walk down comfortably. Kard had installed himself in one of the rear benches and looked both crammed in and surprisingly comfortable.

"A wagon like this carries forty troops," he told Teer. "Weapons are kept on them; personal packs go up."

Teer had only noticed the racks as obstacles to avoid. They could hold rucksacks, he supposed. *Forty* bags would probably require some cramming.

"Any gear beyond knives and repeaters goes in a cargo wagon. One cargo wagon to five troop wagons. A stable wagon for every cavalry troop, though any sane cavalry officer will do everything he can to keep his troop *off* the dragons."

"I can see why," Teer said grimly. "That stable is going to be bad enough for Star on her own. Is that why you didn't buy a horse in Cossax?"

"No time, horses will be cheaper in Shiaray, transporting a horse costs almost as much as buying one, and yes, I knew what the stable on the dragon tail would look like," Kard confirmed. "I've done this before, like I said."

"Three days, huh."

"Versus fifteen or more."

Teer nodded his agreement with Kard's point, taking the bench across from his friend. At least they weren't trying to cram two people into each bench.

A whistle echoed from the front of the dragon.

"Starting up the fires again," Kard explained. "We'll be underway in a few minutes. They'll stop for the night somewhere, probably a military hostel. We'll take Star out for a walk and camp. Our fee doesn't cover the hostel—but if they weren't stopping over nights, we'd be taking half a day less."

"You know how it works," Teer said. He'd been feeling in control and on top of things when he'd managed to keep Kard alive, handle the would-be robbers and get them to town. Now he was feeling inexperienced and lost again.

"Dragons are far from the best way to travel, but they are definitely the fastest."

14

The wardtown of Carlon, along the Carahassee, held the title of largest town in the Eastern Territories. When Teer had been there, he had found the town overwhelming. Everything from the power of the wards raised around the defensive fort to the sheer number of people had been utterly new to him.

But if Shiaray was smaller than Carlon, he was at a loss to tell how. As he and Kard disembarked the dragon, leading Star away from a wagon the horse was *very* glad to see the end of, noise assailed him from every direction. He could see the wards that covered the town, translucent green domes that he'd always assumed everyone could see.

Of course, if everyone else could see the wardline, there wouldn't need to be lines drawn in the ground to mark them for those passing through. People generally weren't too bothered by the wards, but livestock didn't like it.

Teer had driven more than one herd of cattle through a wardline in his time. Above Shiaray, though, he could make out the division between what appeared to be *three* separate wards, each as large as the single ward over Carlon.

He couldn't see what they covered, because the dragon docks were a town unto themselves. Three lines ended at Shiaray and had done so for over a decade. Even Teer knew that there were always discussions of expanding the dragon lines into the Eastern Territories—Shiaray was one of three dragon-towns that sat on the border of the new lands, with the three north, two central and two south lines all terminating roughly where they had been at the end of the Sunset Rebellion.

There in Shiaray, warehouses formed a thirty-foot-tall wall that surrounded the docks. Raised platforms—the titular docks—made it easier to walk Star off the dragon and down a permanent ramp into the roadways.

"Come. There's a hotel I know," Kard told him. The enforced rest of their journey seemed to have finished much of what Nerami had begun, but Teer still watched his friend carefully. There was an edge to Kard that hadn't been there before Shellsvan, and the injury had only aggravated it.

"We'll check for bounties at the wardtower," the older Hunter continued. "But that's after we have a secure place to put our gear. We don't want Star carrying two horses' worth of saddlebags for any longer than we have to."

———

FOR ALL THAT Teer had never heard him mention the town except in passing, it was quickly clear that Kard knew Shiaray well. The hotel he knew was a smaller building down a back street—one of packed earth instead of the flagstone-paved roads where the Unity had expected troops to march—but the staff were eagerly helpful and there was a solid lock on the door to their room, enough to secure their gear while they scouted the town.

The second stop was a horse market. Teer had only seen them at a distance before, but the wardline just short of it led him to suspect why Shiaray had multiple wardstones.

As they approached the horse stables, he took a moment to walk up a bit of raised ground and look east.

The horse market was several large buildings with a corral to exercise the animals. Past that were several more corrals, currently empty, which Teer judged to be part of the market, from the stables attached.

The market alone had to have capacity for five hundred or more horses. Past it he could see rows of empty stables with signs that he figured advertised rental prices. Beyond them was an open field, clearly churned into mud by hooves and feet and dried again on a regular basis, even from a distance. That was where the cattle drivers would camp, and then to the south, there were the cattle pens.

With the pens empty, it took an experienced eye to see them for what they were. They were just squares in the distance, each of them surrounded by fences. There was space there for thousands of cattle—probably *tens* of thousands—and an entire wardstone had been set up just to protect the livestock fields.

He caught up with Kard as the Hunter approached the red-faced man who appeared to be running the place. The horsemaster's coloring was odd to Teer—he had the pale tones of a Shiggan, the most southerly of the Unity's people, but it took Teer a heartbeat to recognize the florid tones of someone who hit the bottle often and deeply.

"Well, be welcome to the market," the man told Kard. "You don't have a beast with you, so you not selling."

"No, I need to purchase a horse," Kard confirmed. "My last steed was killed by a bear while we were traveling in the Latch Mountains."

"Hmph. Ways to walk before getting a new horse." The Shiggan was silent for a few heartbeats, then walked over to a roughly carved desk.

"Drink?" he offered, picking up an unlabeled black bottle and a cup.

"A bit early for me," Kard replied. "Thank you."

"Serves you." A moment later, the cup had to be half-full, and the horsemaster downed most of it in a single swallow. "Need a mount for the young 'un too?"

That had to be Teer, who said nothing in response.

"Nah, *his* horse was smart enough to dodge a bear. Poor mare's been hauling both of our gear since. She's a calm creature, but I think we've used up her patience."

"Smart man to know that's a thing you can do," the local replied. "Some think horses little more than machines. They've got opinions, you know. Not souls, but *hearts*, right?"

"Agreed. I'll miss my Clack, but I'm a Hunter and I must travel. And travel needs a horse."

"That it does." There was a pause as the man filled his cup and took another swallow. Cactus spirit, Teer realized from the smell. The same drink Ohlman, another Shiggan, had given Teer when he'd offered him a job.

That was why he didn't touch alcohol anymore, and the scent brought back uncomfortable memories.

"Name's Rio," the horsemaster introduced himself. "You seem smart enough that you'll know what you're looking for. Lay it on me, Hunter."

"I need a cavalry horse—outrider, not a charger. Strong and tough, with the endurance for the long ride and the training not to spook when a gun's fired from the saddle. Mare or gelding is fine, but I'm not fool enough to ride a stallion into the Territories!"

Rio snorted, staring down at the cup like it held some kind of answer.

"A tenday ago, I'd have horses for you to choose from," he told Kard. "Not many, not this season of the turning, but they were here. But a tenday ago, I had a pair of assistants, too."

He was silent.

"You have horses," Kard pointed out softly.

"But not a one trained to the gun," Rio replied. "Magistrate came through seven, eight days ago now." He shrugged, clearly unsure of the exact time and not caring.

"Tested the horses for gun-shyness in the crudest way."

Teer had never put much thought into that concept. Star had been one of the ranch horses before Hardin had given her to him, and she'd never been bothered by having a quickshooter fired from her back.

He had known other horses that would spook at the sound, though, so he realized what the word meant. And he could envisage just how a Spehari Magistrate could *test for gun-shyness in the crudest way.*

"Took the ones that passed, I take it," Kard said, his tone flat.

"To serve the Unity. And since the Unity protects us all, of course, she didn't pay a shard. Day after, press gang scooped my boys off the street as they were coming here. Thirty-four horses left, even after she took fifteen and three died in her *test.*"

Rio had drunk more than wise. His words were factual, Teer supposed, but the acid of his voice might be enough for a Spehari to take offense. And while things like the Right of Retribution—that a member of any of the Arani peoples who struck a Spehari was to be executed on said Spehari's order—were very clear, they also weren't entirely necessary.

As the Magistrate had clearly reminded Rio, all of the Unity belonged to the Spehari. If she decided it was necessary, she could order the horsemaster's death, and no one would blink.

Kard was clearly thinking something similar, as he stepped up to Rio and took the cup from barely resisting fingers.

"I think you need to sit down, friend," he told the man.

"I'm *fine,*" Rio snarled. "Who even *are* you, that you want a warhorse?"

"A Hunter. I'm in town to buy a horse and pick up bounties. Then we'll be gone. What's the best of the lot you have left?" Kard asked. He still hadn't given the man a name, Teer noted.

Rio fell back into the chair at a push even Teer barely saw.

"They're all beauties, innit they?" he half-whispered, crying now. "And the Magistrate… jus… *killed* three of them to save *time.*"

Teer joined them at the desk and silently took the bottle away. It took him a few heartbeats to find the cork, but he resealed the bottle and tucked it into a box of tack. The man would find it easily enough once he was sober, but it wasn't right to hand.

He knew, without even asking, what the worst part of the Magistrate's sick test had been. The stampede that would have been triggered by gunfire wouldn't have killed all three horses. At least one would have survived, too badly injured to be healed.

Rio would have been forced to put down his own horses, injured in an utterly wasteful stunt so the Magistrate could rob him. Rio would have paid the farms for the lost horses. Without the coin for selling them, that could shutter the man's business.

Someone else would come along. Shiaray was a cattle-drive town and a dragon-town. There would always be farms looking for middlemen to sell horses to the cattle drivers and drivers looking for horses in turn.

But Rio's business might not survive.

"They *are* all beauties," he heard Kard tell Rio. "I haven't even met your herd, but I've known many horses in my time. Some were strong, some were graceful, some just had such great hearts… but they were all beauties in their own way."

Teer had thought he understood anger. His own anger at the Unity had been enough to lead him into a foolish mistake that had nearly got him killed. Abray's anger burned through the memories Storm had stolen.

But something in Kard's soft voice as he reassured a man whose life the Unity had just destroyed—not because they'd needed to, but because it was *convenient*—told Teer he did not begin to know the depths of the rage that filled his friend.

They couldn't keep faith with us, but they should have kept faith with you.

That was what Kard had told him, when Teer had told the whole sad story of his father's pension and the paperwork mess-up that had seen his mother reduced from a comfortable but tight living to utter poverty and desperation.

"May the moons guide them to the Nightmare Sea," Rio snarled. "And my boys… gutting my herd may have risked their jobs, but they still *had* jobs. Supposed to protect them from being drafted, innit?"

"It is," Kard agreed. "I can't do anything about that, friend, but I do still need a horse. Which of yours did you say was the best?"

"Singer," Rio murmured. "She's a black mare, brave as anything but sticks with the herd. She didn't spook at the gunshots; she ran with the herd to protect the others."

"She sounds like a good horse. She's for sale, then?"

"I don't know." Rio looked up at Kard and there was suspicion in his eyes. "What does it matter? She was the boys' favorite, but they're gone now too. What are *you* going to do?"

"I'm a Hunter, Rio," Kard repeated. "I'm going to take her east and find bad people and bring them to justice. I keep people safe, and if she comes with me, she'll help. Right?"

"She'll help. It's what she'd want... I think. I just don't know anymo—"

Kard was closer to Rio but Teer was faster, stepping in to catch the local as he fell from his chair. He quickly checked over the man's pulse and put him on his side to be sure he could breathe.

"He's the look of a heavy drinker, but I don't think he's slept in days, either," Kard said quietly. "We need to get out of this town, Teer. If the Unity is drafting this hard, they've got to be launching a new offensive in the north—and if there's one Magistrate in town for a draft, there might be more."

"We're just going to take this Singer?" Teer asked, a touch horrified —first at the thought, and then at himself for thinking Kard might do that.

His friend was already pulling his purse out and gave him a dark look, his eyes haunted. He poured out its contents and counted up the redcrystal stones as he put the smaller coinage back.

"I'm not sure if this Singer is worth twenty stones, friend," he told the unconscious horsemaster, "but you're not awake to argue, are you?"

He piled the stones up and carefully covered them so no one walking into the stable office would see the money.

"Come on, Teer. Let's find this Singer. If she's half the horse he thinks she is, she'll be easy to find—and Rio strikes me as a man who knows his horses."

15

If Teer hadn't heard a single word Rio had said, he still might have been able to pick Singer out of the herd as the horse they wanted. The door between the barn and the corral was open, allowing the horses to wander as they pleased, but they were clustered together in the building for comfort.

They might not understand everything going on, but they knew that things were *wrong*.

And as the two men approached, there was a visible shift as the larger horses moved to protect the others—and at the head of the instinctive defensive line was a large black mare, her eyes alight with fire as she stared the strangers down.

Both men were familiar with horses and stopped well short of the distance that the herd would register as a threat. All of them, horses and Hunters, waited silently.

Finally, as if some invisible clock had run out, Singer neighed resignedly. The herd seemed to relax a bit, though none of the horses seemed quite ready to dare the corral yet.

"They're lookin' for food," Teer realized aloud. "Rio lost track of time. He's... goin' to be even unhappier with himself once he realizes he missed feeding 'em."

"That's a problem we can solve," Kard told him. "I'm going to have a conversation with Singer. You go feed the rest of them."

Teer knew his friend was quite serious about the conversation. He headed toward the barn, moving in a practiced manner that would spook neither horses nor cattle. There were times, as a ranch hand, that you needed to spook the animals—usually to counter something else that had scared them—but the vast majority of the time, you wanted the big creatures around you to see you as a friend.

This herd hadn't had a good tenday. The Magistrate's test had been cruel, they'd lost herdmates both to the draft and the test, and then the people they'd relied on had disappeared. One of their people remained, but he was in rough shape and the horses would know it.

There were a few concerned sounds from the horses as he stepped into their space, but they seemed to recognize his intent. The feed cupboard was locked, of course, but since it was secured against the horses rather than anyone with hands, the key was hanging on a hook only a few feet away.

It didn't take him long to refill the empty feedbox, though the horses weren't overly patient about the matter and kept butting their heads into his way.

All of the other horses had eaten before he saw Singer again, the big black mare stepping into the barn like a regal queen. The herd parted for her, letting her walk up to the trough and eat her fill without so much as a whinny.

It wasn't until she turned back toward the door that Teer realized she was wearing a halter she hadn't been when he'd first seen her. It was a simple thing, woven together without even a single buckle, and it had a long cloth lead tucked up onto it.

"We had a good talk," Kard told Teer, following her into the barn. "She's coming with us, but she needed to eat and check on her herd first."

"You can talk to horses?" Teer asked, keeping his voice low in case he'd missed someone approaching. "That hasn't come up before!"

"I can't *talk* to them," the El-Spehari said. "But I can share emotions and images a bit. I've never ridden a horse that I hadn't talked to enough for them to agree to carry me."

"Huh. I mostly just feed 'em until they start followin' me everywhere," the ex-ranch hand replied with a chuckle. "Star and I have been together for a few turnings now, even when she was Hardin's."

"And that bond is worth more than my ability to promise Singer I'd made sure Rio wasn't going to break," Kard murmured. "The money we left him will be enough for him to take care of himself and the herd until the new season comes around. And the horses knew that this was a temporary herd, that they'd go to new homes."

He chuckled.

"They may not be brilliant, but they're not stupid, either." Singer trotted up to him and nudged him with her head. Kard reached up to take the lead with no resistance from the horse, then looked at Teer.

"Time to get back to the hotel," he said. "I'll need to do some work on Clack's tack to make it fit her, but she's big enough that it'll be simple."

"I need to stop by a couple of stores and pick up supplies," Teer said. "Meet you at the hotel?"

Kard paused, then shook his head grimly.

"No, Teer. The Unity here is dangerous. Your papers should protect you from the draft, but we've heard a few stories about youths that should have been safe getting picked up anyway. Harder to ignore the papers of *two* Hunters than one."

"Okay." Teer didn't like that thought. Something was just *wrong* in Shiaray, and it grated on him.

"I could find the things I needed to make new arrows in Cossax, but I didn't find the right fiber for the bowstring itself," he told Kard. "I saw a hardware store that looked promising, but I might need to check a few places."

"Fair enough." Kard paused. "Sure you'll know what you need when you see it?"

"I'm mostly confident I could make a bow from scratch, given the tools," he replied. "It would take me longer than Abray, and the first one would need replacing sooner than I'd like, but I could do it.

"Bows were a big deal for the Merik at one point." Teer shook his head. "I'd never even *seen* a bow like this one before, but the lessons I have are from a long tradition."

"It was mentioned in the *History of the Spehari Unification*," Kard pointed out with a chuckle.

Teer had been reading the first book—*Volume I: Landings and the Merik*—of that particularly dense work in his prison cell when Kard had decided to save his life. It hadn't been an easy read for him, but he'd eventually made it through two of the nine volumes.

The third was in his saddlebags, though he hadn't touched it since they'd found Abray's books. *Those* were proving even harder to get through.

"The *History* brushed over the loss of that part of our culture," Teer said grimly.

"The *History* is probably the most honest record of the Spehari arrival the Unity allows to be regularly available, but there are definitely pieces they want everyone else to forget," Kard agreed.

"Come on. Let's go get you a bowstring."

───────

THE HARDWARE STORE that Teer had spotted on the edge of the livestock district, just inside the ward of the main town, was larger than he'd thought it was from his passing glance. It was a massive barn-like structure, with towering shelves that would require ladders to reach the top level.

It took him a few minutes of poking around to realize just what he was looking at: this was the resupply center for the cattle drives. Each of those was anchored on a group of covered wagons that included mobile kitchens and other necessities of life for fifty people on the road for tendays on end.

This store supplied everything they needed to repair and update those wagons—and a set of signs declared that they could arrange custom construction of any type of wagon anyone wanted.

Since the cattle drives were only in town for a half-season twice a turning, the store was likely often quiet, but the chill stillness to the place sent a shiver down his back as he found a section of twines, wires, fishing line and other things that *might* work for him.

Most of the lines were much the same as he'd been able to find in Cossax, but there were a few strings that might work. After testing the feel of several of them, he picked up several yards each of three of the narrowest fibers—two of animal sinew and one plant fiber. Each of the three would work on their own if twisted together, but Abray's memories told him that blending the three might work better.

"Is there no one in this store?" Kard murmured. "We've been here a bit, looking for this section; I'd have expected the proprietor to ask us what we needed."

"If they were closed, they'd have been locked," Teer argued. "There was a counter with a bell. I'll go sort out payin' for this. You go check on Singer."

The horse was hitched outside, though with the simple halter Kard had put on her that was more symbolic than anything else, in his opinion.

There was no one behind the counter when he arrived, and for a moment, Teer thought Kard might be right that the place was abandoned. He rang the bell and waited—he heard footsteps immediately, at least.

After a good twenty or so heartbeats, a panel he hadn't noticed in the wall slid back and someone looked through it at him. It was high enough and discreet enough that they probably thought someone at the counter wouldn't notice it, and Teer decided not to react.

Something was *very* wrong in this town.

The door behind the counter swung open a bit later, a dark-haired Kotan woman emerging. It was unusual to see one of the Kota inside the Unity, but Teer was familiar enough with their blue skin and general demeanor to simply give her a respectful nod.

"Can Milla help you?" she asked.

"Lookin' to buy these," Teer said, laying the fiber strands on the counter. "I was worried for a moment you were closed and I'd missed a sign."

"No, no, Milla's not closed," the woman said, glancing nervously toward the doors. "Milla's boss said to keep head down. *Goods can be replaced, Milla; you can't.*"

She deepened her voice as she quoted her employer.

"Wise man," Teer told her. He gestured toward the fiber. "How much?"

She quoted him a price, and he pulled a few shards out to pay for the potential bowstrings.

"What are you hiding from?" he asked grimly. "My friend and I are Hunters. If there's a problem we can help with, well…"

They were only supposed to get involved in official bounties posted by a Wardkeeper and any problems in Shiaray should have been dealt with *by* the Wardkeeper.

"No one can help," Milla said with a brief flash of a smile. She was older than him, probably nearing thirty turnings… which meant she was still in the age range for the draft, if a recruiter was spreading a wide net.

Except she was clearly employed.

"Unity needs hands, so recruiters are picking them up," she told him. "One of Milla's fellow store clerks is now heading east to serve. Milla would be terrible soldier. So, Milla save everyone time."

"Sounds fair to me," Teer agreed with a forced cheer—and hoped she recognized that his anger was at the whole situation, not her.

She neatly folded the strings, wrapped the whole package in paper and handed it to him.

"You also of draft age, stranger," she warned. "Gray coat not save you. Milla say keep head down."

"I will," he promised. "Thank you."

16

After seeing Milla's unconcealed fear, the streets of Shiaray felt different to Teer. There was noise coming from all sides, yes, but he could see and hear the difference as he followed Kard back toward the hotel.

There was an undertone to the noise, the conversations and footsteps and work that made up the city. A quiet edge that hadn't been there in Carlon. Like everyone was lowering their voices and watching their steps.

And there were almost no young people on the street. A few groups of children, but almost everyone they saw out moving around the city was older, obviously out of the age for the draft.

The feeling was starting to get under his skin. This wasn't *right*. Teer could see the logic for conscription to fill the army. He didn't *like* it—it had taken his father to his death, if nothing else—but he could follow the logic.

But this didn't feel like logic or even planned. This felt brutal, like the recruiters were grabbing everyone without any thought paid to the supposed rules around the system.

He was on edge enough that, combined with the general over-

107

whelming sounds of the large town, a new strange sound didn't register as something to watch until it was too late. He only distinguished the steady *step-clank-drag* from everything else the moment before he followed Kard around the corner to the street holding their hotel.

Right in front of them were a team of Unity cavalrymen, six older troopers with perfect uniforms and cold eyes. Their horses didn't seem any friendlier, and even Singer pulled the two Hunters away from the riders.

Behind them came a sight entirely unlike *anything* in Teer's experience. Another three Unity soldiers, these on foot, each led a chain of youths linked together by ankle manacles. A dozen draftees stumbled after each soldier, the groups only barely able to keep to a steady-enough pace to keep the chain from tripping them up.

Another half-dozen Unity troops, half on foot and half mounted, followed behind to make sure no one tried to get away or fell too badly—though Teer realized he might well be ascribing too generous a purpose with that last thought.

The men and women in the chain were mostly his age. Some were a bit younger, some a bit older, but all of them were at an age where they should have been starting their lives. From the stories he'd heard, most of them *had* been, with workers and even apprentices grabbed off the street.

Kard's warning hand on his shoulder told him his anger was showing—at least through their magical bond. He could feel the other man's anger too, though Kard's was a colder, more bitter and worn thing.

They stepped to the side, off of the main road, as the chain gang was marched forward. None of the "recruits" were looking around. Their attention was on their feet or the person in front of them, their body language exhausted and defeated.

"More riders coming," Teer warned Kard as he caught the sounds of more hooves coming up behind the Army group. The soldiers might have been willing to ignore them if they stayed out of the way, but something in the approach of the new trio of riders told Teer he was going to need his Hunter's license.

The outer two wore the same gray uniform as the other soldiers, but the woman in the middle wore a dark burgundy version of the same tunic and trousers, with a gold chain draped across her shoulders.

The dark colors offset her pale skin and copper-red hair. Blue-green eyes seemed to pierce Teer's soul from thirty paces away, and he *felt* her power in a wave that left his knees shaking.

Kard was one thing. Kard routinely concealed his magical power along with his identity, the illusion hiding his face only one part of a larger glamor that he'd told Teer could withstand even the scrutiny of a Spehari.

It would need to. Teer had lived in the pocket of one half-Spehari for a turning and spent several extremely active days in the company of another, Captain-Magistrate Taran, at Shellsvan. That was enough for him to know that *this* Magistrate was no half-blood.

"That one," she said sharply and precisely, gesturing toward Teer. "He seems good stock. Volunteer him."

The two riders were moving before she'd finished speaking, sweeping toward Teer and Kard with a ponderous sense of inevitability.

But Kard was there, inserting himself—and Singer, though the horse following him only added bulk to his living barrier—in front of the riders.

For a moment, Teer thought the cavalrymen were about to ride Kard down. Then the big black mare gave a sharp neigh of a kind he'd only heard from herd matriarchs before, and both horses, trained cavalry mounts who should have only obeyed their riders, stopped short.

"What is the meaning of this?" Kard demanded, glaring up at the riders as if he didn't care about their mounted height.

"Anyone of seventeen to thirty turnings without a clear job or apprenticeship is subject to call-up at the recruiter's discretion," the righthand soldier said briskly. "The recruiter has decided your friend is subject."

"My friend, like me, is a licensed Hunter of the Unity, which renders him exempt from the draft," Kard told them flatly. "Besides, you seem to have your hands full already."

He waved to the chain gang moving down the street.

"This lot will hardly fill a single wagon, Hunter." The Magistrate's voice sent shivers of something down Teer's spine. She pulled her horse up behind her guards and looked down at Teer and Kard with curiosity.

"I have a dragon tail with six hundred seats to fill, and trainers at Fort Leyyan waiting for two thousand souls," she continued. "The safety of the Unity demands it. Shiaray, like the rest of our great nation, will send forth her best."

"And Shiaray will need Hunters to help the Wardwatch keep the peace afterward," Kard said reasonably. "We have a job to do here, sah."

She *smirked* down at him. Teer wanted to shiver, but he suspected that drawing her attention was a bad idea.

"Your name, Hunter?" she drawled.

"Akelis, Magistrate. My companion is Teer."

"Sergeant Bakir, their papers," she ordered.

Teer only had the one set, with his proper name. He hoped that Kard had one under the Akelis name, because the only ones *he'd* ever seen for his friend were for Kard.

And while Kard wasn't the El-Spehari's actual name, he'd only ever heard the name *Karn* a handful of times.

The cavalry trooper who'd spoken before dismounted, his face twisted in disgust like the ground itself offended him, then walked up to Teer and Kard, holding his hand out in silent demand.

Teer gave the man his license, hoping he wasn't about to join the chain gang that had just rounded the corner—headed toward the dragon docks. To the very dragon they'd arrived on, from the number she'd given for empty seats.

The trooper didn't read the two pieces of paperwork. From the way he looked at them before stepping back to the Magistrate and handing the licenses to her, he quite possibly *couldn't*. Cavalry troops often came from ranches like Teer's stepfather's, and only some ranch kids were taught to read.

"Carlon and Vester," the Spehari said, flicking through the documents. "Quite a ways apart for the two of you to be traveling together, no?"

"I'd been a Hunter for turnings before my cousin here needed work," Kard replied with a shrug. "Took him on as a favor, but he proved an able hand, hence Wardkeeper Ashan giving him his own license when we brought a gang in."

"An entire gang, with just the two of you?" Sergeant Bakir scoffed.

"We had a local guide for help," Kard said.

The Magistrate laughed, a warm, velvety sound that could make a man forget she was part of the race of tyrants that ruled them—and probably two hundred or more turnings old, on top of that.

"I have heard similar stories before, Sergeant," she told Bakir. "From Hunters, in my experience, they're usually true. Return their papers and let these fine Hunters be on their way."

"Of course, Magistrate Mona."

The soldier handed their licenses back, almost as if touching the papers was hurting his hands, then swiftly remounted.

Mona, for her part, eyed Teer and Kard for a few more moments.

"I am Lady Mona of House Ghee," she told the pair. "I will have use for Hunters in the next few days, I believe. Many are those who are attempting to hide from their duty to the Unity. A list will be posted before we leave. The Wardkeeper will see you informed."

"We will speak with them before we leave," Kard promised. "As Hunters, of course, we mostly pursue paid bounties."

"If money matters, you will receive it. I leave that to the Wardkeeper," Mona said with an airy wave of her hand.

That appeared to be the last she was going to say, as she turned her horse and urged it up to a canter after the chain gang.

A turning before, Teer had drawn a gun on Kard in anger and nearly destroyed his own life. Without that experience, that certainty of doom if he tried to shoot a Spehari mage, he wasn't sure the presence of armed bodyguards would have been enough to keep his quickshooters holstered as the woman rode away.

Worse… from the emotions coming over their bond, he wasn't sure that Kard would have stopped him if he had drawn.

17

Knowing how a thing was done and being able to do it were two frustratingly different things. Teer hadn't really anticipated better, but he'd hoped to make better progress than he did.

He'd wrecked over half of the cords he'd picked up before he finally managed to braid the strands together into a bowstring that met the minimum expectation from his memories.

Kard was out bonding with Singer, leaving Teer to work through the manual tasks of preparing his bow for use on his own. He knew he'd need help to actually *string* the bow—the arms were naturally bent in the "wrong" direction for proper use, and it would take two to get it into position for stringing.

He tied one end of the string to the bow for easier storage, then turned to arrows. Thanks to Abray's reserve, he had twenty-five arrowheads, but none of the shafts were usable. They gave him the length and weight he needed, though, and he'd spent time in and since Cossax breaking blocks down into rough shafts.

He laid one of Abray's arrow shafts out next to his blanks and began to shape them down to match. Everything from the angle of the wood to the depth of the notches for the arrowhead and fletching was carefully measured, he knew, and Abray had used specialty tools for much of the work.

Teer had a knife.

But he was also a Merik Adept, and thanks to Abray's memories, he had some sense of just what that meant. He could carve with a knife to a precision few others could match.

It was slow work, intensive and almost meditative. Wood shaved away, he tested the feathers he'd acquired and the old arrowheads, and then he carefully shaved more wood away until he finally had an arrow he could use.

As he grew more comfortable with the process, it sped up, until he had a dozen arrows lying in front of him and his mind began to think of more than just the task before him.

There was only one place his mind could go. A chained-together group of young people, people who might have been his friends if he'd grown up there, forced down a street with little care from their taskmasters.

The party he'd seen had to be only one of several—dozens, from what Mona had declared. Six hundred souls. Six hundred innocents, caught up in a net for no greater crime than being around when the Spehari had decided to find soldiers.

He *knew* how his father had been drafted. It had been a measured and coordinated process. Even faced with an open rebellion by the El-Spehari, it had been handled by the local Wardkeeper. She had, according to his mother, called out everyone in the fishing village of the right age and held a lottery.

A village of five hundred souls had seen a hundred youths gathered before the wardtower—and only twenty of them had been called up the day Teer's father had gone to war. Before the Sunset Rebellion was over, two more drafts had been held, sending another twenty of the young fishers to war.

He supposed six hundred of ten thousand was a smaller part of the town, but the manner had been so different. He'd never been under much illusion that the Unity's laws applied to the Spehari, but there were supposed to be laws and promises around who would be called up for war.

Not this process of scooping random people off the street, regardless of whether they were needed where they were. This was horrific—and more, when his father's village had put forty of five hundred into Unity service, the Unity had faced a dire threat, with open warfare being waged by a rebel faction of fully trained Mages.

Teer wasn't sure he could have walked by the type of draft the Unity was *supposed* to have. But this? The supposed soldiers-to-be marched through the city in chains like slaves?

This was wrong.

That thought brought him to the last arrowhead and he looked down at the tarp he'd laid out to catch shavings. Twenty-five arrows, each longer than his arm. The bow itself, a relic of a part of his culture he'd never even known existed.

He wasn't sure when he started laying out his weapons. The black-iron longsword went next to the bow, with the Kott-steel saber next to it. He was drilling with the longsword and could use it better than the saber, but he knew the Kott-steel sword had a presence in his dreams that had helped guard him from Storm.

With a Spehari Magistrate in the city, he wasn't sure if the black-iron blade had enough similar properties for him to put aside a weapon that had helped him so well.

Two quickshooters, each with a silver handle and a hardened steel barrel. They were solid guns, nearly masterpieces of their type.

His hunter *was* a masterpiece, with blued steel and carefully aligned optics. The breechloader was meant to be what its name implied: a hunting gun, not one used for the field of battle. For all that, it was the gun he'd first killed with, taking down a bandit leader when the man drew on Kard.

Next to the rest of the small armory, the short repeater looked old and worn. He, Kard and the Kotan Shaman Tyrus had put it together from the best parts of several guns, creating something that looked a lot less solid than it truly was. Teer took good care of the weapon, too, knowing that his life could depend on whether its mechanism could keep up with his speed of fire.

It was a lot of weapons, more than he could really carry at once. He'd have to take a look at his saddle to work out how best to store them—or possibly even put some of them into Kard's larger-on-the-inside saddlebags with the El-Spehari's spare weapons.

The stack of guns didn't really give Teer an answer for how to deal with Mona's dragon loaded with conscripts… but that he was looking at them at all told him he *was* going to be doing *something*.

———

KARD RETURNED to find Teer seated on his bed, most of his gear packed back into the saddlebags he'd take down to the stable in the morning. The younger Hunter's weapons were still spread out on the bed next to him, and he was considering what he knew about the draft.

"You look thoughtful," his mentor said. "And dangerous. With a Spehari in town, this isn't the time to raise our heads."

"Kard." Teer wasn't entirely sure what he was going to say, but he met the El-Spehari's eyes and smiled grimly. "I have the memories of thirty turnings of the seasons in exile. Half of a lifetime longer than my own.

"Abray lived decently for what he became, but he was an exile. Even when he was fallin' in love with a woman in Cossax, he limited his visits into town from fear. Once Opal moved in with him, *she* did almost all of the shoppin' in town.

"His entire life for thirty turnings was shaped by fear and hidin'. I remember *all* of it." Teer shook his head as he knew suddenly what Abray's ghost had wanted from him.

"Since enterin' your service, we have danced around the edges. We have saved people, yes—Lora, but also everyone Storm's clan would have killed, given time. We have fought alongside the Unity, and we've found Hunters in the same damn coats we wear.

"But in the end, we have hidden, and what I have done with you is protect the Unity."

"We protect the people," Kard argued, but there wasn't much heat in it. "It's not much. I *know* it isn't much, Teer, but I don't have it in me to do less... and I can't risk doing more."

"I can't hide anymore."

The words hung in the room like a challenge.

"I *can't*," Teer repeated. "Not with Abray's memories in my head. Not with the knowledge and the skills he left me. I can teach other Merik to use these gifts, but we both know that the Unity won't let that stand. Not unless we're real careful, hidden and safe."

He shook his head.

"To teach what Abray knew, I would have to ask others to swear the oath he swore," he told Kard. "*I will shield against the darkness. I will guard the innocent. I will uplift the humble.* I can't ask others to swear that oath if I can't live up to it myself. I understand, now, why Abray didn't teach in his exile.

"Because he broke that oath by hiding. Not by running—he *had* to run—but by hiding. By never challenging what the Spehari were doing to the innocent and the humble.

"If I let *six hundred* souls be chained and dragged off to fight in a war they know nothing about, what am I? Am I still the protector I imagined myself as when you got me my Hunter's license and coat?"

"Be careful of the path you set your feet upon," Kard told him. It wasn't an argument, Teer realized, only a warning. "You can't fight the Unity. For all of your gifts, I'm not sure you could fight a single Spehari. Magistrate Mona could kill you with a gesture and a word."

"I know," Teer agreed grimly. "I suspect she'll find me harder to hurt with her magic than she expects, but I will likely only have one chance to take her down. But I *can*, Kard. And those poor bastards she's marching onto that dragon in chains? What chance do they have?"

"None." There was a long pause. "A regiment of two thousand draftees will have a battalion of steady troops, volunteers and second-term veterans under Marked officers attached. They'll march behind… and they'll shoot down any soldier who runs."

Teer shivered as his friend's description.

"You know this," he said flatly. "Because you commanded regiments like that."

"Yes." The single word was all Kard said for a moment, but Teer's burning gaze earned him a shake of the head.

"The draft was smaller before the Rebellions," Kard said. It wasn't a defense. "We had a thousand volunteers and veterans to fifteen hundred conscripts, not five hundred to two thousand. That change was brought in *against* us.

"We reorganized the Sunset Brigades even before the Rebellions, based on the experience of those of us who had led regiments and brigades in wars," Kard continued. "We'd learned that splitting out the troops like that was terrible for everyone's morale. It made the draftees feel like they were fodder—and it undermined the integrity of the blocking battalions, too. Teach them to think half of their companions are inferior, and it will rot a soldier's soul.

"Merging them at the company, even the platoon level, evened them out. Gave us veterans in every formation to steady the new recruits, whether they were volunteer or conscript."

He shook his head.

"Of course, doing that requires you to *trust* the troops, at least a bit. I'd rather have a soldier run before the battle than during it, though. Even conscripts were owed respect, pay and pensions."

Teer shivered. The last was what had been taken from his family because the draft records had been lost.

"And this draft? What's going to happen to *them*?" he demanded.

"I don't know for sure," Kard admitted. "But most likely, they'll spend a season at Fort Leyyan, being broken and remade. At the very least, they will learn that if they fail, they will be punished.

"Then they will be put on dragons again—probably not in chains at that point, but having known the Spehari like Mona, that may not be certain—and sent north. If they're pulling six hundred conscripts from Shiaray, they're probably mustering at least ten new brigades.

Fifty thousand troops, a major push to retake the Kott mines and foundries.

"Why open new mines and build new foundries in the Unity, after all, when the Kott already have them?" he asked bitterly. "Much of the current lot were built with Unity knowledge, if not resources, so there are those that can argue that industry belongs to the Spehari anyway."

"Will it work?" Teer asked.

"No. The Kott were part of the Unity once. Every type of gun and cannon the Unity can field, the Kott have too, and the Kott know their swamps better than any army the Spehari can take north." Kard stared grimly off into the air. "There's a reason that the Sunset Rebellion ended fifteen turnings ago and the war against the Kott continues. If they send ten or twenty brigades north, they'll lose half of them at least.

"You can't stop that, Teer. You'd need to, I don't know, storm the training forts and free the conscripts there."

"I can't save everyone, I know," he agreed. "But I think we can save *this* six hundred. I think I have to try."

"It's not just a matter of breaking them free, you know. There are documents listing the name and home address of every one of those conscripts. They are supposed to get paid, after all."

Teer rolled that around in his head in silence for a moment. "Where?" he finally asked. "How many copies? My dad's records were *lost*, after all."

Kard smiled coldly, his expression showing he might sense the same weakness Teer did.

"They can't send records through a wardstone," he agreed. "One copy will be here, kept with the Wardkeeper. The other will be with Mona. If you can't handle *that* copy, your entire effort is doomed. It's the Wardkeeper's copy that will haunt them, even if you succeed."

To Teer, Kard's illusory appearance as a Merik related to him was only visible if he focused. Most of the time, it was something closer to a cloud of orange motes floating around Kard's actual body and face. A face that could pass for Spehari to anyone who didn't know better.

"I can see options," he said quietly. "But I won't drag you into this, Kard. This is a weight I must face, not you."

"There is saving my life in a fight, which you've done a few times now," his mentor told him, his voice just as soft as Teer's. "And then there's pulling my unconscious body from the aftermath, sewing up my skin, *making an antivenom from scratch* and hauling me to a doctor to finish the job."

Teer… hadn't really thought of what he'd done as that much more than he'd done before.

"We look out for each other," he told Kard. "That was the deal, as I figured it. You saved me from the gallows, so I watch your back."

"We are so far beyond you repaying me for *anything*, Teer, that I don't even have words," his friend replied. "Some days, it seems like the only thing you've asked me for since then was to give Lora a chance."

"I am set on this path, Kard."

"I know."

The two of them sat in silence for a moment, then Kard sighed and pulled an oddly shaped piece of leather from inside his coat. It had a clear inner side that glittered with red in a way Teer had never seen before.

"This is a gift; I'd been making it for a bit, but looking at that pile of weapons, you need it."

Teer took it and flexed it slightly before realizing it was a saddlebag that hadn't been cinched up yet.

"Here's the cord." Kard passed that over as well. It had the same length and style as the ropes on Teer's existing saddlebags, but the fabric was softer and also had a crystalline reddish tinge.

"What… is this?" Teer asked softly. He carefully ran the cord through the ringed eyelets cut in the leather, pulling it up into a proper saddlebag shape.

"Extra space," his friend told him with a chuckle. "You had to unpack my bags to find the medicine to treat me, so you know mine are magic. This is one of them. There's about fifty stone of redcrystal in there, between the bag and the cord, which tells you everything about why my people want that crystal so badly."

Teer blinked down at the leather bag in his hand.

"Kard, I…"

"It was from the callipsus money Taran gave us," Kard told him. "And you need it, if we're going to keep going the way we're going—let alone if you're going to wage war against the Unity."

He shivered at the description.

"I don't want to wage war against the Unity," he admitted. "But I can't stand by and watch injustice happen like this. What else can I do?"

"Hide." The stark admission surprised Teer, though he knew it was the case. "Become like Abray was. Or like I've been. Hiding away, letting fear of the Unity define who can be, even after we've broken with them."

"I can't."

Kard walked over to his bed and took the saddlebag from his hands. Loosening the cord, he opened it up to show that the interior now looked quite different. There was no trace of the crystals that had been ground up and glued to the interior. Only an open space, easily large enough for everything Teer currently had spread across half a dozen saddlebags and several equipment attachments on his saddle.

"Technically, you are bound to obey my commands," the El-Spehari told him wryly. "We both know I've never tested that because I'm quite certain your Adept gifts would prevent it anyway.

"Pass me the Kott saber."

The sudden change surprised Teer, but he passed over the sword, sensing—either from the words or through his link to Kard—that the other man needed to speak.

18

*K*ard lowered the scabbarded saber into the bag and pressed it against the interior lining. Teer watched as he pressed his fingers into the lining and then pulled out a piece of it to wrap around the scabbard's top.

The blade hung solidly from the side of the saddlebag's interior, drawing easily without moving the scabbard when Kard tested.

"Fifteen turnings ago," Kard finally said, then shook his head. "Nightmare Sea, no. *Twenty-nine* turnings ago was when it all began. The Prince in Sunset was given an army and the mission to bring the Kott into the Unity *at any cost.*"

Teer realized he knew very little about what had started the Sunset Rebellion. He knew that his father had died in the war. He knew that hundreds of thousands of others had died in it too, and that Kard had served at the right hand of the Prince in Sunset, the Governor of the Sunset Territories. He didn't even know where the Sunset Territories *were*, beyond "north."

"Abarra—the Prince—was given five veteran brigades and the right to recruit new troops as he needed from Zeeanan, Loridan and Owah lands," Kard told him. Those, at least, were names Teer knew: tribes to the north of the traditional center of the Unity in Merik lands. The Zeeanan were directly north of the City of Pillars, where the Spehari had landed. The Loridans and Owah were east of them.

"He took *at any cost* literally," the older man continued. He took the short repeater in its scabbard and repeated what he'd done with the saber, attached it to the inside of the saddlebag in a way that left it easily reachable once the bag was open.

"*Any cost*, after all, meant that there was no specified way of bringing the Kott in. Abarra took half a dozen El-Spehari and a single battalion of veteran soldiers into the swamps to talk to the Kott Princes."

Teer took the bag from Kard. He tested the attachment of the two scabbards, discovering that he could pull off the bit of lining wrapped around the cases easily enough, but unless he was touching it, it wouldn't give at all.

He experimented with it, attaching his quiver, moving the position of the sheaf of arrows around and attaching it. He wasn't sure how he'd use his bow and arrows yet, but he wanted the arrows easy to hand.

Plus, it kept his hands busy while he waited for Kard to work through whatever was going on in his head.

"The Princes didn't meet with him initially," Kard finally said. "They knew he came on the Unity's behalf, and it is the task of the Princes to speak for the Kott and protect the Kott. Surrendering to a strange nation would be contrary to that.

"He wasn't the Prince in Sunset then," he noted. "Just Lord General Abarra. But to speak to the Princes as an equal, he had to be a Prince. There are trials and challenges and rituals that a Kott must pass to become one, and once he put his feet on that path, enough of the Kott were willing to help him that he could move from task to task as he completed it, with us backing him up."

Kard sighed.

"You've seen both Taran and Mona now," he noted. "You understand the sheer presence of my father's people, of even us half-bloods.

Now realize that Abarra was something *more*. As a half-blood, he had more presence, more *power*, than many full-blood Spehari.

"Their trials and challenges weren't designed for Spehari. Things that would be the edge of impossible for a Kott were easy for Abarra —but things that a Kott would find merely difficult were enough to bring him to the edge of death.

"But he succeeded. The Kott recognized him as a Prince and he met the Princes as an equal. He offered them a deal. They would enter the Unity willingly and be brought under the protection of the Spehari.

"The technical and industrial knowledge of the Unity would be shared with them. They would pay taxes and provide troops, like anyone else, but their status would be special. The details took three tendays to agree, but Abarra did what no one had done before: he brought an entire people, millions strong, into the Unity by diplomacy."

"What went wrong?" Teer asked, unable to resist. He could feel the old grief and anger in his friend now.

"When the Spehari said *at any cost*, they really meant *no matter how many Arani die*," Kard said bitterly. "A cost in knowledge and power and position? That was far less acceptable.

"Initially, the King in Winter hailed it as the great success it should have been. Abarra became the Governor of the Sunset Territories— named for the Kott's name for the Spehari, the *Sunset People*— including all of the Kott lands along with chunks of the Loridan and Owah lands.

"I think the intent might have been for him to see how the Loridans and Owah were governed and realize that this was the *right* way to govern Arani," he continued. "Instead, we started implementing something similar to the deal with the Kott in the non-Kott parts of the Territories.

"We started to be able to raise volunteer troops at levels most of the Unity couldn't manage with a regular draft. Taxes, in redcrystal and iron and the resources that keep the Unity functioning, were up.

We were building mines and foundries, and we thought we were building an example that would show the Unity the way forward."

Kard was staring at the wall now, and Teer wasn't sure if he should ask a question or just let his friend talk.

"Then the Magistrates started coming in. We were being overruled on internal postings. The Prince in Sunset—the Kott started calling him that before we ever knew it had a meaning in Spehari prophecy, because he and his people 'came from the sunset'—went from hand-picking his subordinates and even raising Arani to lower-tier Magistracies to having them imposed on him.

"And even among the Kott, those Magistrates started to impose the ancient so-called Rights of the Spehari. The deal to bring them in was being disregarded at the highest and lowest levels, with the Prince stuck in the middle, trying to see his word kept."

Teer could only barely conceive of a part of the Unity run the way Kard was describing. He'd spent his whole life in the Unity as he knew it, a Unity where Mona's draft in Shiaray was unusual but not unacceptable to the vast majority.

"It was the Right of Retribution that wrecked everything in the end," Kard murmured. "That was why I couldn't stand by when you were arrested, you know. I couldn't watch it happen again.

"I don't even know what the Magistrate was doing. She was a problem, one we'd been trying to pull up short, but she thought she had the backing of the King in Winter. She might have.

"All I know is she got on the wrong side of a Kott Prince who thought they were protecting their people from her. They fought. One of the other El-Spehari Lord Colonels managed to intervene before either was killed, but you've used a Kott Prince's blade. The Prince drew her blood, and she demanded their life."

Teer shivered, remembering the chaos around his attempt to shoot Kard. Kard had tried to let him go, but the Unity had been cracking down on anti-Spehari sentiment. There had been a standing order that applied to him and would have seen him held for the Spehari Magistrate—who would have executed him, if for no other reason than to spare himself the energy required to charge Alvid's wardstone.

"To the Kott, everything Ssolss did was not just acceptable but correct, their charge and duty as a Prince. To the Spehari, it was a crime that made their life that Magistrate's to claim—and she demanded their head. The Prince tried to speak to his grandfather, to negotiate a counterproposal, but while he was tied up trying to speak through a wardstone, she commandeered a battalion of newly arrived troops and attacked Prince Ssolss's home."

Kard turned back to Teer and shrugged.

"I arrived about a candlemark too late to save them," he admitted. "I had to pull together a regiment of troops I could trust and the backup to handle a Spehari.

"Whether her troops or mine truly fired the first shots of the Sunset Rebellion, those shots were fired around Ssolss's home over whether they deserved to die for defending their people."

"It sounds like you knew the answer to that question then," Teer said.

"Lord Colonel Karn *knew*, with a passion few could match, that protecting others was the right thing to do. He'd listened to Abarra for too long, seen a gentler hand work too many times, to embrace the harsh rule the Unity believes is needed."

"And Kard?" Teer asked.

"Kard had to hide to live. Kard watched the King in Winter spend *fifty thousand soldiers* and burn half of his own city just to bait the trap that brought his grandson to the Court of Pillars." He shook his head.

"And then I watched the King I had once believed was the future of *every* people kill his grandson, who I *knew* then was the *better* future, with his own hands and magic. I tried to honor Abarra's last command and get his people to safety."

There was a haunted tone to Kard's voice now.

"I failed, Teer. I got two Lord Colonels and maybe eighty soldiers out of the City of Pillars. There were ten of us El-Spehari with the Prince and almost sixty thousand Sunset soldiers in the city.

"I got *two* of my brothers and eighty troops out. *Eighty*."

"And now you think I'm asking you to go back to war," Teer realized aloud. "I can do this on my own, Kard. You can leave, get to safety before I kick off a hornet's nest."

"No." Kard finally turned to face him, and there was a strange calm in his face. "No, I can't. I *won't.*

"So, I hope to the Pillars, my young friend, that you have an inkling of a plan."

19

They rode out of town the next morning with just that on their minds. The road to the east was a well-maintained military road, part of a network laid out between key forts. The farther they got from Shiaray, Teer knew, the worse the road would get until it was merely a packed-dirt track kept mostly clear of brush.

They weren't going to ride that far. Shiaray was built where areas came together. Dragon lines came in from the west and the south. A river—far smaller than the Carahassee but enough to give the town and the cattle drives water—ran out of the mountains through the northern third of the town.

To the east, prairie stretched off into the distance, and to the west, rolling forested hills swept away toward more "civilized" lands. The forest around Shiaray itself was long gone, consumed by the unending appetite of a major settlement for lumber, but there were enough trees to mark the razor-straight line of the military road.

"Here," Teer said, as they had the road to themselves for a few minutes. A carriage, making excellent speed with a team of six horses, had just passed out of view ahead of them, and the closest person behind them was barely visible to him.

Kard didn't say a word, just urging Singer to the side and leading the way into the trees. The forest was thin enough to be easy going for the horses, but Teer had to hope it was enough to hide them from people on the roads as they turned back to loop around Shiaray.

"From what the Wardkeeper said, the dragon will be leaving tomorrow night," Kard said once they couldn't see the road. "He wasn't sure why, but I'd guess they've got another batch of draftees coming in from the Territories. There was certainly enough talk of the press gangs making sweeps through everywhere, not just Shiaray."

"Meaning Mona's six hundred are *after* people like her have already grabbed everyone they could easily pick up in the town," Teer guessed.

"Exactly. This kind of mess is just… bad practice," his friend noted. "Makes for unreliable troops and disloyal towns. But it gets you bodies this turning, and it makes the point of who is truly in charge."

Kard paused.

"Looking back, I wonder if the second half is more important to some of the people at the top," he continued grimly. "Especially hitting somewhere like Shiaray and the Eastern Territories, where there's always going to be a strong streak of independence."

Teer didn't respond. There wasn't much point. He didn't really need to understand *why* the Unity was doing what it was doing. He'd decided he wasn't willing to let it stand, and that was enough.

"Why tomorrow night?" he finally asked, considering the distance and the ride ahead of them. They not only needed to get around Shiaray without being seen, they needed to reach the dragon line and follow it to find a spot for an ambush.

A spot where two men could fight sixty or more.

"Presumably, whoever they're waiting for isn't expected to arrive today—or they're expecting them late today," Kard said. "And with draftees, they'll always leave just before dusk. It gives them time to organize them onto the dragon tails while it's light, and the darkness will help discourage anyone from doing anything foolish once the dragon is moving."

It would make their ambush both harder and easier in different ways. Teer could work with it.

"We need to get ahead of them," he declared. "Let's up the pace."

———

Just getting around Shiaray without getting close enough to risk drawing eyes took the entire day. Twilight was falling, giving Teer shivering memories of the Latch Mountains, when they finally found the cleared path through the trees marking the dragon line.

He didn't remember this particular bit of woods from their journey the other way, though he'd probably looked at it. Pulling Star up, he took a long glance along the line, searching for an obvious weakness.

The two lines of iron were attached to wooden crossbeams, presumably as much spacers as anything else. A gravel bed had been laid around and over the beams, creating an even surface for the lines to run along.

At first look, the lines were one solid piece, stretching off in the distance to either side without a break.

Since that was impossible, Teer dismounted and walked over to them, crouching to examine the iron. Even from that distance, the line appeared to be a single piece of metal, but as he paced along away from Shiaray, he began to see the discolorations. Every fifteen feet or so, there was a region of the metal track that had a dark tinge to it, the dirty gray of the iron faded toward a burnt-brown color.

"Were these bound by magic or some tool I don't know?" he asked, looking back at Kard.

"Magic. It's part of why the lines haven't been extended since the Rebellions," his friend said. "The last stretch of eastern dragon line was planned and budgeted before the war started, so the King pushed it through—but a dragon line takes a season or more of a skilled Spehari or El-Spehari mage to complete."

"And it was mostly the El-Spehari doing the work, wasn't it?" Teer guessed.

"Exactly. After the Midnight Proclamation, the Unity has a lot fewer Mages to go around, and the King in Winter has higher priorities for them than fastening metal beams together."

Teer ran his finger along the metal, marveling at how smooth the connection was. Without knowing that the line *couldn't* be one solid piece for miles upon miles and looking for the connecting points, he wouldn't have been able to tell.

Which created a very real problem for him.

"How do we break it?"

Kard grinned.

"What was made by an El-Spehari mage can be unmade by an El-Spehari mage," he replied. "Tomorrow and farther from town, I think, but I can tear the lines to pieces whenever we're ready."

"Good." Teer nodded, looking around them. "You're right; we want somewhere farther from help and preferably more restricted. This won't be a good ambush point."

"If they're smart, they'll watch more carefully at the good ambush points," Kard warned. "But they're not going to be ready for us."

"Let's set up a camp well back from the line." Teer whistled softly and Star trotted over to him. "We have some work to do to be ready, either way."

———

ONCE THE FOOD was finished and the dishes were clear, the two men set to the task of stringing Abray's bow. Teer at least knew how it was *supposed* to work, but Kard had never strung a bow in his life. He'd worked with Kota who'd used them, but while their bows were of the same basic design—made of wood, sinew and horn, with the ends reversing when unstrung—they were smaller and lighter.

"I think we need to be less careful with it," Teer finally admitted, looking down at the Merik warbow. So far, they'd managed to get it bent in the right direction but not far enough to string it. "If it can handle this in use, it has to be able to take it while we're stringin' it, right?"

"So you say," Kard agreed, glaring at the weapon with clear irritation. "If I didn't *know* that a silent weapon is going to be very useful tomorrow, I'd say this was a waste of effort."

Teer chuckled and gestured for Kard to take the center of the bow. Still slowly, but not gently this time, they pulled the arms of the bow back with all of the supernatural strength available to them both.

Finally, Teer was able to hook the other end of the string into its place on the bow. He nodded to Kard to release the weapon, trying not to cringe at the potential injury if the bowstring snapped.

But it held. His careful braiding of the strands had done what his memories insisted it should, creating a cord with enough strength and heft to serve on a warbow built for a man of incredible strength.

Kard held out his hand and Teer passed the bow over. His friend ran his fingers along the wood, then took up a decent archer's stance and tried to draw it.

It was clear he'd seen archers shoot often enough to have some idea how it worked, but the bowstring barely moved under his fingers.

"I'm not quite willing to spend more energy on magic just to draw this," Kard said wryly, passing the bow back. "And I can tell I'd need to. Good luck."

Teer had kept half a dozen wood blanks—carved into shafts and fletched but lacking in points—for practice. Now, with the camp cold for the night, he stepped away to take a few practice shots.

Despite Kard's inability to draw the bow more than an inch, Abray's drills came easily to his mind. The string moved easily under his grip, though he recognized how much strength he had to use to move it.

Taking up one of the practice arrows, he picked a tree and walked through the process. Nock the arrow, rough aim, draw to the ear, precise aim, release. He didn't fire the arrow the first half-dozen times, just working through the motion to tell how it felt.

After half a dozen repetitions, he knew that he wasn't going to be trying to fire the bow at speed. *Abray* could—he had memories of the other Adept emptying a twenty-arrow quiver in a few minutes in a battle—but he would need a lot more practice.

And more calluses.

The seventh time, he drew the arrow back, aimed at the tree and released. The shaft flew straight and clean, piercing the trunk even without a point.

He'd hit higher than he'd been aiming—he knew the arrow would drop more than a bullet and had overcompensated.

He wasn't sure whether he could afford to practice too much. Even with healing trances and similar tools learned from Abray, he could tell that pushing himself on this could hurt him. The bow was a lot to work with.

But he was going to need it, so he nocked another arrow.

20

A storm crackled away across the mountaintops, and a distinct scent wafted through the air. Teer didn't know where he was standing for a moment, before the memory crashed in. The ruins around him had once been a collection of utilitarian stone structures, though draped in all kinds of greenery and tapestries.

All of that had been burned away and several of the buildings had exploded when gunpowder stocks had been set aflame.

There were no fires in the monastery buildings as Teer stood there, nor was there any scent of smoke or death. It was the monastery as Abray had last seen it, but without the clear marks of fire and death that had marked it then.

Teer caught a sound behind him and turned quickly, drawing a sword instinctually. Looking down, he realized it was the Kott-steel saber Kard had given him—once again manifesting itself inside dreams that weren't dreams.

"This seemed the right place to meet."

Abray's ghost was waiting there. He wore the black-iron longsword Teer had found in his chest over his back, crossed with a quiver, and his warbow—the same one Teer had been practicing with before he slept—was slung over his shoulder.

Despite wearing weapons he hadn't carried in ten turnings by the time of his death, Abray looked like he had at sixty turnings. More of a grizzled mountain hermit than a martial master.

"I didn't expect to see you again," Teer admitted. "From what you said, you weren't going to last long."

"I said I'd last long enough." The ghost shrugged. "And it turned out there was one more factor I hadn't considered, anyway." He reached back to tap the sword. "I am more Abray now than I was when we first spoke, oddly. The sword you've carried is more than you think it is. Its power and yours have sustained Storm's construct.

"I remain what I am," he warned. "I am still a weapon forged to destroy you. But because I am forged of Abray and because you are an Adept, I have no need to do so. I have, in fact, been able to smooth the struggle with his memories.

"You'd have found a reconciliation eventually, I think. You are a young man of extraordinary will. That is what I saw in you when we spoke before. And I see it again now, shining far more than it did then.

"You have made your choice. You understand the path that you must walk, and you have chosen with your eyes open.

"I told you that you could be what I wanted you to be," Abray reminded him. "And that you knew what held you back. Your decision and the path you have taken were a surprise to me in some ways. I will admit I did not expect the El-Spehari to not merely allow it but to join you.

"He does not walk the Adept's Path, as you have chosen, but his own path is not without virtue. Together, you may be able to change more than the fate of a few hundred—but you understand now that you must try."

"I do. Would you have me swear your oath?" Teer offered.

He didn't even sense Abray moving. Suddenly, a steel chain was draped across his shoulders.

"The chain is a reminder, that we are always bound to service first," Abray told him. "It is not necessary to carry it but to understand it. You do."

Now the construct held out the black-iron blade.

"Like the sword you are holding, this exists here," he warned. "Both have different powers and strengths, but they are tools worthy of the wielder, if you can be worthy of them.

"Take the sword, Teer. And with it, take what I can no longer be. The memory I can no longer use. The essence of what made Abray a Master of his path."

Teer sheathed the saber and took the black-iron blade. Something shivered through him, and he didn't even need Abray to ask. The words came to the lips of his dreamself instinctively—a memory from Abray, a message from the blade… and a choice from him.

"By this, my chain of steel," he declared, running his free hand along the chain of dreamsteel he wore.

"By this, my sword of iron," he clenched the blade. He knew that it was something strange, something valuable, but it was now his and he was its. He didn't know what that meant, but it would have to be enough.

"By these, the fires of my skill." His free hand clenched over his heart. Dream or not, this all felt *very* real. "I do swear upon my magic."

He felt that power answer the call, a smooth flow of magic that ran through him. He knew that the cuts he'd inflicted with the bowstring would be gone when he woke up.

"I will keep my word unbroken.

"I will shield against the darkness.

"I will guard the innocent.

"I will uplift the humble."

Things he had always tried to do, even before he began to realize that he was anything strange. Just a ranch hand with a horse and a gun, he'd never wanted to be anything but a protector and a friend to those in need.

"I will strike with only mercy.

"I will kill with only need.

"I will wield my magic true.

"I will strive to do no harm."

The two parts of the oath were opposed, Teer knew, and he also knew that it was the *balance* between the two that was critical. To protect could require violence, but it couldn't be the first choice, and an Adept, stronger than most they would face, also had to know when to *stop*.

"I will teach those willing to swear this oath.

"This I swear upon my chain.

"This I swear upon my sword.

"This I swear upon my magic."

Thunder rolled across the monastery, and the scent of air after the storm faded. Abray was gone. The black sword was in Teer's hand, and he realized the bow was now slung over his shoulder.

You choose the Path, another man's voice said in his head. *A worthy sacrifice. I will show you the way.*

21

They rode west along the dragon line in the morning, looking for the right place.

Teer knew they'd traveled along the same route aboard the dragon only a few days before, but he was surprised to realize how different everything looked when you were moving at the pace of a horse versus the pace of a dragon. He knew the steam-powered machine had tripled the best speed Star could make, but he hadn't accounted for how much that would have warped his image of the scenery outside the wagon windows.

But some landmarks stayed the same. He gently pulled Star to a halt, looking at the tallest of the hills and matching them to his memories.

"We're close," he told Kard. "Not sure how close, but the hills are looking like what I remember."

There was a particular rocky valley he remembered, a cut through one of the steeper hills carved with explosives and magic. There was space on either side of the lines there but not much. Enough to leave the dragon tail if necessary but not enough to offload the conscripts in an organized and supervised manner.

Enough space for Mona to try to deploy her troops, Teer figured, but still narrow enough to funnel the troops with the Magistrate into the fire of two men.

"There, I think," Kard agreed, gesturing toward the rockier hills ahead of them. These were less heavily forested than the hills where they'd stayed with the Kota, far to the east from there, but the trees were taller with thicker trees and branches.

There was plenty of cover to hide within—and almost as many roots for the horses to trip over if they weren't careful.

When they reached the cut, it came out of the forest almost suddenly. The line had been rising gradually for a few hundred yards, but at some point in the past, it looked like half of the hill ahead of them had collapsed. That mass probably formed the gentle rise they'd been riding up, but the slide had created a steep rise forty feet tall.

It wasn't insurmountable for a person on foot, but even a horse would have trouble getting up it. There was no way the dragon line could have made that angle, and the Spehari designers had clearly decided going around the hill was too much effort.

The line continued on the same gentle rise it had been following before, cutting into the face of the hill in an artificial pass about forty feet wide.

The pair of them rode along the cut, following it as it rose up until it finally matched the level of the hill and turned to descend again along a gentler natural slope.

"About three hundred yards," Kard noted, turning Singer at the top and looking back along it. "If I had to move troops along this, I'd send a cavalry sweep out in advance to make sure it was clear."

Teer hadn't considered that, but it was manageable.

"We'll need to wait until the cavalry sweep turns back before takin' out the line," he suggested aloud. "Can you do it that quickly?"

"It'll be more obvious, and we might not be able to get the pieces far enough away to prevent them fixing it," Kard warned. "Mona might not have built a dragon line before, but she's Spehari. She's smart enough to figure it out if she looks at the intact lines for a few minutes."

"What happens if the cavalry don't report in?" Teer asked, disliking the thought.

"Depends on their orders," his friend admitted. "If they were to ride ahead and meet up at the next stop, only reporting in if there was a problem, the dragon will still move on time. If they were to report back either way, we might have a problem."

"How can we tell?"

"They'll be earlier in the day if they're supposed to report back no matter what. If we see them a couple of candlemarks after noon, they're going to check back in once they've completed their route—and we might not be safe until we see them ride *back*.

"If they show up closer to dusk themselves, we don't need to worry about them doubling back, but we may have less time for the work either way."

Kard shrugged.

"We wait and see when they arrive," he said. "Make our call then. If we haven't seen by the time the sun starts going down, I'll wreck the line, and we'll deal with riders if they show up ahead of the dragon."

"You know how they work," Teer allowed. "Too many lives are on the line. We do it carefully, but we can't fail."

"Agreed. Speaking of, any thoughts on how to deal with the Wardkeeper's records of this draft?"

Kard seemed to be leaving that one entirely in Teer's hands, which was… irritating. On the other hand, Teer *did* have a plan.

"Oh, I realized that's actually easy," he told his friend with a grin. "You're going to walk into his office tomorrow afternoon and ask for 'em."

There was a long silence.

"Fuck," Kard finally said. "Late enough that they know something might have gone wrong, early enough that no real Magistrate will have arrived."

"You *were* a Magistrate. You can say the right things to convince the Wardwatches to hand over the record of the draft."

"I probably can," Kard agreed. "That has a lot of potential to go wrong—there *are* other Spehari in Shiaray—but it's so simple, it will probably work. So long as I have backup in case of trouble, anyway."

"All of this is my idea. You'll have backup," Teer promised.

———

THEY SET up a rough camp half a mile back from the cut, as much to put the horses somewhere safe as to rest. Singer's examination of the knots as they walked away told Teer that they probably didn't need to worry about the two mares if something happened to the Hunters.

He'd intentionally tied a knot that he knew Star could work free of in a day or so without even realizing it. He wasn't entirely certain Singer wasn't capable of *undoing* the knots on her own.

Star was clever for a horse. Clack had been similar. *Singer* was something else again.

With the odds Teer had decided to face, the thought was actually reassuring. Whatever happened, Star would be fine.

Returning to the cut, Teer set up near the top of the gouge cut through the hill, on a higher patch of ground that gave him a clear line of sight down the entire three-hundred-yard ravine.

He had the black-iron sword, the warbow, his quickshooters and his short repeater. Kard, settling down next to him to watch the area, was carrying quickshooters and his own short repeater, along with his Kott-steel saber.

It didn't seem like enough to face what Kard had estimated to be two full platoons of Unity soldiers. The troops assigned to a press gang would be solid and reliable too. Veterans that Mona trusted to do dirty work.

That didn't, Teer hoped, mean they were very good *fighters*. He wouldn't plan for it, but he could hope.

They'd left their heavy gray dusters in their saddlebags and wore dark clothing that helped them hide in the trees on their rise, watching for signs of the cavalry Kard figured was scouting ahead of the dragon.

"There."

Teer had better eyes than Kard, but the older man knew what he was looking for. Once he'd pointed out the movement of foliage and birds, Teer saw it as well. He couldn't see the riders through the cover, but there was a pattern of change.

"Timing isn't right," Kard muttered.

Teer hadn't checked the time, more focused on watching for the coming threat than anything else. They weren't planning on taking down the scout patrol, but it could end up being necessary.

I will kill with only need. He'd let them ride past if he could, but if it was a choice between killing the riders or not being able to stop the dragon, he'd do what was needed.

"They're too late to be expected to report back, too early to be riding all the way to the next stop," Kard continued. "Something's not right, Teer, and that's—"

"A problem." Teer finished.

He drew his repeater from the scabbard across his back, knowing from its weight that it was loaded. Dropping to his stomach, he moved forward to be able to cover the cut.

Whoever was coming split to either side of the dragon line, and Teer could see that the movement was wrong.

"Those aren't professionals," he murmured. "And... they're not on horses, Kard."

The ridge that had required the cut was too sheer for trees, and the strangers emerged from the forest below them. They were moving in good order, but they definitely weren't Unity cavalry.

They'd also clearly been expecting the ridge, as they didn't even slow before starting up it. It wasn't a particularly difficult ascent for people, a steep hike rather than a scramble. It was only horses and dragons that couldn't go up it easily.

When the newcomers had reached the top of the ridge, they were still over two hundred yards away. Teer could see them in detail, though, and he had no idea what he was looking at.

There were about thirty of the strangers, split into two uneven groups moving along the cut. All of them were armed, with a mix of hunters and what Teer judged to be older full-length repeaters. They didn't wear anything resembling a uniform, dressed in a random mix of town and country clothing.

Then he recognized one of them with a start. She had switched into what he recognized as traditional Kotan war-dress—close-fitting trousers and a corset-like top—but Milla's blue skin made her stand out from the group and drew a second glance.

It was definitely her.

"That's the Kota clerk from the hardware store," he whispered to Kard. "She didn't strike me as a soldier. What is goin' on?"

"Rebels. You weren't the only one Mona's press gang was the final line for," Kard said grimly. "I see a few who look like hunters and foresters. They know these hills, which means that they're either going to find us or that we aren't in as good a spot as we thought we were."

"Then we should get ahead of that."

Without waiting for Kard to reply, Teer put his gun away and rose from the ground.

He walked out into the open toward the oncoming rebel company, his hands clearly visible. He had a better-than-decent chance of being able to draw the quickshooters and open fire before anyone could shoot him, though against thirty gunhands, he'd be doomed no matter what.

"I recognize one or two of you all," he said loudly as he saw he'd drawn their attention. "And I don't think you're out for a casual stroll in the woods any more than I am. Shall we talk?"

There were suddenly a *lot* of guns pointed his way. As he'd seen from the distance, it was a mix of hunters and repeaters, though closer in, he saw that there were half a dozen thunderbusses in the mix as well, and most of them wore a quickshooter at their waist.

"And who by the mountains' stone are *ye*?" a beanpole of a Shiggan man demanded. He was one of the foresters Kard had picked out, Teer judged, clad in a hard-wearing hide jacket over similar denim trousers to everyone else.

"I am Teer. In normal days, I am a Hunter, but a long time ago, a press gang dragged my father off to a war he didn't come home from,"

Teer said calmly. "And watchin' folk like me get dragged through the streets in chains, well, that didn't sit right. Came out here to see if I could do somethin' for 'em."

"I'm guessin' you lot had much the same thought."

"And I'm supposed to just take ye at yer word?" the Shiggan demanded.

He was the loud one, but Teer wasn't convinced he was in charge.

"We're half a day's ride from Shiaray, all of us gathered around the best place to ambush a dragon for thirty miles in either direction," Teer noted. "You folks aren't out here for a picnic, and neither am I."

He and the forester faced each other down. There were still plenty of guns pointed in his direction, though Teer noted that only a few were still aimed directly at him. The Shiggan man was one of those still aiming his weapon, a well-kept hunter, at Teer.

"Milla met him in town," the Kota woman said, stepping up next to the loudmouth and putting her hand on his barrel. "Don' know if he Hunter, but he were *angry* at the draft."

Teer gave her a small nod.

"We're both here for the same reason," he said. "Stop the dragon, kill the Magistrate, free the conscripts. I had a plan, but I didn't have this many hands. You got a better one?"

"Not many would say aloud that they were going to take on a Spehari, son," a new voice said. A hooded woman who had drawn no notice amongst the group stepped forward and threw back her hood to reveal her face.

She was Merik, her face marked with a nasty scar along her left cheek where a bullet had nearly taken an eye. Older than either of the two Teer had been talking to, her streaked-gray hair was cropped short, and she'd concealed herself even there in the forests.

Somehow, none of that took away from her presence once she threw the hood back.

"You're in charge here," Teer said. He wasn't asking.

"As much as anyone," she agreed. "But Agus here was raising all the questions I wanted to—and he makes for an excellent challenge. Thank you, Agus, but I will take it from here."

The tall Shiggan forester didn't even blink. He'd already lowered his hunter at Milla's interruption, and now he slung the weapon and stepped back. Gestures called several of the other rebels to him, and he seemed to be in charge of at least part of the plan.

"You weren't alone here, Teer," the stranger said. "You should call your friend out. I think we're past the risk of violence, no?"

"I can never be too sure." Kard emerged from the bushes—significantly closer than Teer had thought he was, even with their bond— and from the position of his repeater, he'd had Agus covered the whole time he and Teer had been staring each other down.

"The lad can be charming, but once he's decided on something, his mind is hard to change. I just try to make sure he lives through his mistakes."

That *very* much fit the image of the "older cousin" Kard's current face projected, and Teer just chuckled.

"I didn't catch your name, ma'am," he told the woman.

"I have many," she replied. "But you can call me Song."

Song saw something in Kard's face and grinned.

"Yes, Hunter, *that* Song," she confirmed. "And yes, that, too, was a test. I'm intrigued that you didn't recognize the name, Teer."

"I let my cousin look through the bounties," he said with a shrug. "There are types of bounties we don't take."

"And after a few turnings of the season, you can tell when the Spehari are lying for their own reasons," Kard said calmly. "Usually when the stones on offer are more than the official crimes would ever justify. Robbery and battery and assault and suchlike, sure, but they never did hang any deaths on you, did they, Song?"

Teer took a half-step back to stand next to Kard. He didn't even look at his friend, but he knew Kard could feel his questioning thought through their link.

"She's an agitator and a rabble-rouser, Teer. She finds trouble, then makes it bigger. Helps sometimes, sometimes makes things worse."

"Always trying to help," Song said, but she didn't argue with Kard's assessment. "As I am here. A lot of folks were angry, but someone had to be the one to stand up and ask what we were going to do about it."

"A platoon of untrained rebels against two platoons of Unity veterans," Kard said. "You better have a plan."

Not least, Teer realized, because *his* plan had depended on Kard being able to use his magic. Working with anti-Spehari rebels would be a bad time to do so.

"We do. Can you help?"

"We will help," Teer promised. "That's why we're out here."

"All right. Milla will fill you in on the plan," Song said, gesturing to the Kotan woman, who hadn't stepped away yet. "I don't know your skills, so you'll have to find your own place in the groups.

"We can't afford to get this wrong."

22

$\mathcal{E}$xplosions echoed over the hills, and Teer hoped that the dragon was still far away. It hadn't yet really started to get dark, so they *should* be, but he couldn't be certain. The lack of a cavalry patrol was worrying him, though it was reassuring to be posted up with three other snipers.

One of them was Agus, who seemed to have decided that if Song said he was fine, he was fine. Agus's hunter was the best rifle of the three foresters, almost a rival for the long gun Teer had left in his pack.

"We can probably rustle up another hunter for ye, ye know," Agus told Teer as he watched him check his arrows, "rather than using that antique."

"I *have* a hunter with me. I brought this instead. When you three open fire, everyone within a mile is going to know the fight has started. Whereas this"—he tapped the lacquered surface of the old bow—"can nearly match the range and is silent."

Agus nodded, looking over the warbow with intrigued eyes.

"A hunter can hit a man from half a mile," he noted. He didn't sound argumentative, more curious. "Can ye really shoot one of those arrows that far?"

"No chance," a second forester—this one a Zeannan named Sooill. "I hunt with bows for food; you couldn't hit a man at a hundred yards, let alone three hundred!"

"I couldn't shoot an arrow half a mile, no," Teer conceded easily. He gestured to the dragon line beneath them, where a dozen mine charges had broken the line in multiple places. "But even with this clear shot down the cut, we've only got about three, four, hundred yards of clear sight.

"I can put an arrow into a man at four hundred yards, and while he might live, he won't be getting back up on his own."

His own confidence surprised him. He had a single practice session with the bow. He knew his own gifts as far as matching his speed and precision between his eyes and his hands, but he was still learning the bow.

Except as he tested the bowstring's pull and the arrowheads, he knew he wasn't. Abray's memories were top of mind, as always, but he wasn't following them step by step the way he had been before.

His fingers and hands knew the steps as well as those memories did. Something had changed since his practice session last night—and he knew what it was.

He sent a silent *thank you* to whatever remained of the Abray construct. Created to turn Storm's "gift" into a trap, the entity had purified the old callipsus's weapon and transformed it into a true gift.

"Really?" The forester who said he hunted with a bow was looking at the warbow with a measuring eye. "What even is the draw on that thing? A hundred and twenty pounds?"

"I... have no idea," Teer admitted. He wasn't even sure what the forester *meant* by the weight—it wasn't a measure the Merik Adepts had used for their warbows. They'd made few enough bows that the only measure that mattered was whether the archer it was meant for could draw it five times in a minute.

He held the bow out to the Zeeanan forester, who took it and tested the string. He didn't even attempt to draw it all the way. He tugged on it, then passed the bow back to Teer with a slow nod.

"I don't think I've ever seen a bow like that," he admitted. "You must be mighty strong to pull it."

"Some of it's technique," Teer said, but he couldn't argue the point. Strength wasn't the main advantage his Adept gifts gave him, but he knew that even other types of magic needed to actively use their power to match his strength.

Of course, from what he could tell, his magic couldn't affect much outside his body. If he'd been a Kotan shaman, he wouldn't have needed Nerami to save Kard's life.

"How long until we're expecting the dragon?" the third forester asked. She was a dark-skinned Merik woman who barely came up to Teer's shoulder. Her eyes were cold agates, and she carried her hunter with a precision that he had to respect.

"A candlemark or so after dusk," Teer told her. "I'm keeping an eye open for scouts. I was expecting to see cavalry patrol the cut to make sure it was clear. That's something we'll have to deal with."

"We did deal with it," the cold-eyed woman replied. "Song led me and a few others out ahead. Five riders won't be reporting in ever again."

Teer had been forced to accept a certain degree of necessity with regard to death around him and even by his own hand. He didn't *like* it, and even without the oath he'd sworn, he'd always tried to find ways out that didn't require death.

The woman didn't sound like she regarded the deaths of the cavalry troop as necessary. She sounded *pleased* by it.

"I guess that does answer that," he conceded carefully. "We wait for the dragon now."

Below them, the close-in team—now including Kard—set to moving warped and wrecked pieces of dragon line away from the trail. Once the debris had been cleared away, there shouldn't be anything left of the dragon line at the top of the cut.

Teer hoped that the Dragonmaster would see the missing rail before the dragon hit it. He wasn't sure what would happen to the passengers if the dragon hit the missing line at full speed, but he doubted it would be pleasant.

He didn't want to hurt the very people they were there to rescue, but there was only so much they could do in the dark.

His own plan had called for removing the line by magic and potentially bringing down part of the cut's walls to make a visible barrier. By joining Song's company, he'd given up control, and he wasn't sure he liked the feeling.

An odd thought, he realized, for someone who had followed Kard since the El-Spehari had saved his life. He'd challenged and pushed Kard here and there, but the decisions before the last few days had always been Kard's in the end.

Something had changed when Kard had nearly died in the Latch Mountains—and it wasn't Abray's memories, because those had been in his head for half a season by then.

No. This was *Teer* changing. Abray's knowledge and the conversations with the construct of him were a push, a shove toward a direction he had needed to go, but this wasn't Abray feeling twitchy at following orders.

But for an extra thirty guns, Teer didn't see much choice. Determination and magic could handle a lot, but their chances of saving the conscripts were far better combined than separate.

23

*I*t was well past sunset, and the darkness was settling in heavily across the mountains. Teer could still see down the artificial gorge that the dragon line ran up, but he was starting to wonder what the plan was for everyone else.

His plan had relied on the fact that he and Kard would have an advantage over the defenders. Magistrate Mona was the only one aboard the dragon who would be able to match their vision in the dark.

Given how much else Song seemed to have planned for, though, he had to give her the credit of presuming she had a plan for that. Probably something to do with the packs of chemicals and explosives half of the company had been carrying—the charges that had wrecked the dragon line hadn't been all of it.

Even without his supernatural vision, he suspected he would have been able to pick out the dragon's approach. The brilliant lights that had cut through the fog when the machine arrived in Cossax were only brighter and clearer in the dark, gleaming eyes of glass and magical light.

The beams from the redcrystal lamps at the front of the dragon swept along the cut as the machine entered, the tail of linked wagons rumbling along behind it. Teer exhaled a breath and nocked an arrow to his bow, raising it and aiming without drawing.

A part of him quailed as he recognized Dragonmaster Gerg in the dragon's cabin. The man had been perfectly polite to him and Kard at the time, but there was no real question: the Dragonmaster had known what his dragon would be carrying back west.

Like the soldiers serving in the press gang and now standing watch over the recruits, Gerg was probably not a particularly bad man. But he was knowingly part of what Teer needed to stop.

All of that ran through his mind in the same moment that the Dragonmaster clearly saw the missing lines ahead of his vehicle. He yanked on a lever and *something* changed, machines moving in a way that Teer didn't understand that unleashed a horrific squealing sound.

The dragon slowed sharply. Teer watched Gerg get thrown forward by the force, but the man kept his hand on the brake lever as he forced his dragon to a halt. From the outside, Teer saw that no one inside the tail was going to be unshaken, but the Dragonmaster's sharp eyes brought the dragon to a halt with half a dozen yards to spare.

Then the man started reaching for other levers, likely ones to throw the machine into reverse, and Teer moved. The arrow came back to his ear almost without thinking, and he looked across a hundred yards of night and saw Gerg's professional determination.

He shifted his aim and loosed. The arrow snapped through the night in perfect silence and hammered into Gerg's bicep instead of his throat. The dragon's window didn't even shatter as the arrow punched through, and Gerg's arm was yanked away from the controls and pinned to the back of the cabin.

Teer had a moment to hope that the man was smart enough not to try to pull the arrow out before Song's alchemical solution to the darkness lit off. A dozen matches struck a dozen fuses and rockets blazed into the sky.

Each broke apart a hundred yards up, unleashing glowing fireballs that hung in the air, suspended from some kind of cloth wing.

As the rebels rose up over the edges of the ravine to find their uniformed targets, the distant valley was as bright as a summer afternoon.

———

CHAOS ENSUED. There was a pattern and a form to it, one that Teer could follow, even only knowing half the plan. A second set of mining charges went off behind the dragon tail, collapsing the cut in on itself to make sure the dragon couldn't back up.

Shooters rose up on both sides of the cut, everyone in the rebel group who'd brought a hunter but didn't have the skill to land shots at several hundred yards. They began a steady pattern of shots—not yet aiming at anything in specific but still putting bullets into the wagons of the dragon tail.

That would help keep people's heads down while the main clearing group, led by Kard and Song herself, moved in on the front of the dragon. They were the ones with thunderbusses and repeaters, moving wagon to wagon to clear out the Unity troops guarding the conscripts.

Teer spent a moment to watch as Kard led the way into the dragon itself, repeater pointed at Gerg. Like the rest of the clearing team, Kard was masked to avoid recognition, though his illusory face couldn't be linked to much.

He held Gerg at gunpoint as he gently detached the arrow from the back of the dragon—leaving it embedded in the Dragonmaster's arm—and swiftly tied the man's hands before passing him back through the group.

Even Teer couldn't hear distinct words through the gunfire, but he got the gist of Kard's order: *Move prisoners somewhere safe. Don't take out the arrow until he's at a healer.*

Then he was distracted by movement farther along the dragon tail. The inevitable response was taking shape. Three Unity troopers burst from a wagon in the middle, repeaters lifting to their shoulders as they aimed up at the edge of the ravine.

Teer drew and fired another arrow in a single movement, his

muscles flowing with the newly acquired memories. He hit the long repeater in the hands of the lead trooper, the arrow punching through the barrel and tearing the entire weapon from her hands.

The stock hit the woman in the head as it broke free, sending her collapsing bonelessly to the ground. Gunfire echoed around Teer as the other snipers took their own shots.

They weren't shooting to disarm, and the other two troopers went down with equal suddenness. The three defenders had fired a single shot between them, and Teer hadn't heard anything suggesting that anyone had been hit.

The clearing team was through the dragon and the support wagon directly at its back. While Teer knew there were people in there, he hadn't heard any gunshots from that end of the dragon tail, suggesting that they were using blades or the crew had surrendered.

A trussed-up figure being pushed out of the dragon to join Gerg suggested the latter—but Teer's attention was pulled away by a sudden crash of gunfire from the third wagon. He couldn't see what was happening, but the shooting lasted a dozen heartbeats before that part of the dragon was silent again.

More soldiers were starting to spill out of the wagons farther back, and Teer focused on them. At this range, he was in no danger from them and focused on disarming the people he could.

Like he'd told the other snipers, anyone hit with a shot from his warbow wasn't getting back up quickly. He was aiming for weapons and limbs, but he was grimly aware that even that was only going to make sure *most* of the soldiers he shot lived.

Half a dozen troopers went down to his arrows, and another dozen to shots from the hunters around him. Over twenty of the Unity troops were down, most in the same area of the dragon tail.

That had to have been one that the guards were staying in. There might be another twenty troops in the wagon, but they could also have divided their strength up along the tail.

There was more gunfire toward the front of the dragon, but Teer could also see that someone was starting to urge disheveled youths off of the wagons. Those prisoners were the entire point of the ambush, and he was delighted to see them.

The next round of gunfire announced a problem. None of their people had reached the wagon halfway along the tail—Teer realized in passing that it could easily have been the one he and Kard had traveled to Shiaray in—and the gunfire coming from the vehicle was too measured for a close gunfight.

One of the perimeter shooters screamed, a sound that cut off horribly in the middle. The wagon was being used as cover, and the soldiers were firing up at the cliffs.

There were too few shooters along the ravine walls for them to stand up to counterfire for long. Teer didn't know what Song's plan for that was, but he knew their options were limited.

"Keep this up," he told the others.

Agus started to open his mouth to question what Teer was doing, but Teer was already moving. He wrapped his bow as he ran, sliding it back into its spot on his quiver—and sealing the quiver to protect his remaining arrows. Both movements were almost impossible at speed, even for him, but he didn't want to lose his weapons.

By the time he reached the first of the cliffside shooters, his hands were empty, and he bounced past the woman without a word. The living wouldn't tell him where the enemy were, though the point of his rush was to *keep* them alive.

He slid to a halt on his knees next to one of the side shooters as the man collapsed. The rebel was still alive, but without attention, he wasn't going to live long. The bullet had gone through his chest, and there was worrying froth as he coughed.

There were other people shooting at the wagon holding the troops for now, and Teer was the only one close enough to save the man's life.

He hadn't met this rebel before. He was a pale Rolin man, with graying brownish hair and watery blue eyes—eyes that looked at Teer with desperation.

"Move with me," Teer ordered, gently moving the man into a sitting position as he pulled his knife out. There was no time for gentleness on the next part, and he sliced the man's shirt away from the wound. The fabric seemed light, but it resisted the knife more than he expected. The shirt had been expensive.

Teer had one Kotan poultice on him and several other bandages. Anything clean would work for what he needed to do next, though, and he grabbed a strip of cloth from his pouch. The outer layer of the roll couldn't be trusted, and he pulled it away before pressing the rest against the wound.

Three strips of tape across the bandaging held it in place, sealing the man's lung when he breathed in and still allowing airflow when he exhaled—or so it had been explained to him by a ranch hand when he'd been fifteen.

Abray's training for the battlefield treatment had called for the same kind of bandage, but had focused on *what* he needed to do, not *why*.

The man's breathing seemed to ease a bit.

"Thank you," he gasped, staring up at Teer with a mixture of awe and gratitude that made him uncomfortable. He knew—and so did the rebel, he was sure—that the bandage was a temporary patch that was meant to get the wounded man to a proper doctor.

He nodded to the man and turned his attention back to the dragon. The whole affair had given the man a chance to live and had taken less than a minute.

But in that minute, the situation had grown a lot worse. There was no one shooting from the top of the cliffs around the back half of the dragon—Teer suspected most of them had simply gone to ground rather than being hit, but the real damage was done.

Unity soldiers were moving out of the carriage they'd been firing from. They'd torn the solid wooden benches out and were using them as cover to take up a decent firing formation.

The other snipers on the high ground were pressuring the Unity troops, but the range was long enough for the solid wooden panels to do a surprisingly decent job of stopping bullets. It wasn't perfect— even as Teer was taking in the situation, one of the foresters got a round past the impromptu shields, and a trooper flopped to the ground in boneless silence.

There was a clear ongoing fight in the middle of the dragon tail, pushing back toward the rear where a solid body of twenty-plus soldiers was forming up.

The important question was answered when an older soldier offered his hand to help a burgundy-uniformed woman step gracefully down from the dragon tail. Mona looked around the artificial gorge, blocked to the east by a landslide and to the west by the continued fire of the rebel snipers and the advancing ground team.

Even Teer wasn't sure where the Spehari produced the hunter from. It had either been concealed somewhere on her or she'd magically brought it to her hands from wherever it was hidden.

Ignoring the incoming fire, she lifted the gun in a perfect target-range stance and fired. She reloaded the breechloader with the sure movements of a practiced gunhand, and Teer didn't even need to look at the snipers he'd left behind to know that one had been hit.

He was watching her as the surviving snipers took their shots and saw exactly what he'd expected: blue light sparked in the night as the bullets landed on a defensive shield like the one Kard had used against Teer seasons earlier.

Teer wasn't certain if she'd surround herself with the shield, and that was the only chance he saw for anyone at that moment. He drew his repeater, chambered a round and went prone on the edge of the cliff.

Focus. Release a breath. *Fire.*

He saw no reason to hold back. Seven shots rang out in as many heartbeats, the lever moving under his hands with practiced speed. There was a *reason* he'd built his gun from the best parts of several others.

Nothing less than the best could stand up to his shooting.

His first three shots were into Mona. Then, seeing the first bullet vanish into blue sparks of magic, he switched his aim. The senior noncom who'd helped her down from the wagon went down. Two of the shield holders followed before his last bullet smashed into an expanded shield.

To his eyes, a blue dome now covered the Unity formation on the closer side of the dragon tail. It lacked the scale of the barriers raised by a town's wardstone, but it was more than enough to stop bullets.

And it clearly didn't consume all of her energy and focus, as she gestured toward Teer's firing position. He was already rolling to his feet and moving before she'd completed the gesture.

He had seen Kard and Taran unleash their full power on the callipsus clan that had stormed Shellsvan. That had been a deadly confrontation, one he'd only survived because a portion of Kard's power had been dedicated to protecting him.

Bolts of fire—blue and white to his eyes, though he suspected they might look different to someone else—smashed where he'd been lying and half a dozen feet in either direction.

He was faster. He loaded a single round into the repeater as Mona's fire tore up the top of the cliff, coming to a kneeling halt for just a heartbeat and firing directly at her.

Unsurprisingly, her shield blocked the shot—and this time, she struck with a bolt of lightning that moved *far* faster than the relatively sedate spray of fire.

He was far enough away that it didn't hit him directly, but the blast from the lightning strike picked him up and hurled him away. He found himself scrabbling at the edge of the cliff, about to slide over the edge, and could hear Mona's laugh.

"Shoot him," she ordered.

Fast and agile as he was, Teer wasn't fast enough to dodge bullets—or agile enough to get to safety when the ground itself was trying to collapse under him.

24

The moment seemed to last forever. Teer had just enough control left that he knew he could get back onto the cliff instead of falling thirty-odd feet to the ground—but he also knew that a dozen repeaters were rising up to shoot him and that he couldn't even drop fast enough to avoid the fire about to hit him.

Then a screaming whistle tore through the night as someone lit a flare rocket. Instead of blazing into the sky like the ones still lighting the battlefield, it traced a nearly flat arc to explode into Mona's shield, its fuel and flame scattered across the dome of Spehari magic.

The explosion of fire nearly blinded Teer—but it did the same for the Unity troops, their shots either never firing or going wide. It would only buy him moments against troops with repeaters, so he did the only thing he could.

He moved with the sliding soil and stepped off the edge of the cliff. More blindly fired bullets hit the dirt above him as he fell, and he had just long enough to wish he believed in any gods worth praying to.

Teer knew how to manage falling from a horse, but this was something entirely different. He hit the ground hard, even with trying to bend his knees to absorb the impact, and fell forward. He rolled with the fall, managing to come up onto one knee a dozen feet along the cliff from where he'd been standing before.

Everything hurt, but nothing seemed to be broken. His repeater was somewhere in the dirt, and a still-burning dome of magic blocked him from the Spehari who was going to kill him and everyone who'd joined him on this cursed stupid mission.

Mona's dome of power seemed to explode, hurling the bits of rocket and fire in a dozen directions. She strode out of that chaos, every inch of her *glowing* with power as she led her soldiers forward.

"Find the rest of the scum," she barked. "None of them— Pillars of Iron, that fucker is alive."

She'd seen Teer a moment after he'd seen her. Her shield around her soldiers might have exploded, but he *knew* she was still shielded against gunfire. There was no point in trying to find his repeater or drawing his quickshooters.

He charged.

A blade is more dangerous than you think. An old memory—Abray's memory—of a trainer. *Even without being an Adept, you can draw and close faster than many expect. Anyone unfamiliar with a blade will underestimate just how far you can reach.*

Mona stared at him in complete shock as the black-iron longsword swung from his back and he crossed the dozen yards between them.

Shocked or not, she was a Spehari war mage. She didn't have the time to cut him down before he reached her, but she conjured a shield of force. To Teer's sight, it was denser than the shield she'd summoned around the troops, an almost-solid barrier made of blue sparks of magic.

Teer knew, looking at it, that even he couldn't strike with enough force to break the shield. But he was entirely committed, the charge and the draw all part of the same movement that sent the yard-long blade snapping down in a blow that should have cleaved her head in two.

Mona flinched backward, a full step away from him even as her shield swung around to block his blow—and that flinch saved her life as the black-iron sword cut through her magic like it wasn't there.

The tip of the blade sliced across her face, drawing blood that shimmered in the light of the flares and the moons, almost as bright as her hair.

Teer stepped forward to control the blade, barely conscious of a Unity trooper charging him with a bayoneted repeater. He sidestepped the man and cut gun, arm and shoulder in half with a single strike.

The trooper went down hard, his life's blood ebbing out into the dirt as Teer and Mona glared at each other in the dark. He barely registered the sniper shots that passed his head, taking down the next pair of too-brave soldiers.

"No one has *ever* cut me," the Magistrate snarled at him. "How *dare* you?"

"I am not yours to command," he told her. "I am not bound by your laws or your tablets of prophecy. I judge you for your crimes and your crimes alone."

He moved forward, but this time, she was expecting it. Like the hunter earlier, he never saw her draw the cavalry saber. He *did* feel the impact as his sword hit it, biting deep into the steel of her blade as she parried.

Her saber was probably ruined, but it had done what she needed it to do: stop his next strike so she could gather her magic. Lightning flashed out from her free hand, and there was no way he could dodge it this time.

Pain tore through him as every part of his body screamed that he was on fire, and he was flung back with the force. He hit the ground and his body refused to move, a harsh tingling sensation freezing his muscles as he tried to muster his strength and mind again.

"I am *Spehari*," Mona snarled when she realized he was still breathing. "For my blood, *you will die*."

A second blast of lightning formed around her hands and blazed toward Teer—but it never reached him. It hit something in the air and stopped, orange sparks swarming out of nowhere to smother it before it reached him.

"No."

The single word somehow cut through everything. The chaos had faded; the shooting died down to nothing. The surviving soldiers behind Mona had fallen back, hiding from a steady rain of bullets from the remaining shooters.

A sharp and cold wind seemed to carry Kard's word down the cut as the first group of flare lanterns ran out of fuel. The light noticeably dimmed as the El-Spehari stepped down from the dragon tail, his illusion dropped the moment he'd conjured a shield to protect Teer.

Power rippled out from him, and for the second time in minutes, Magistrate Mona of House Ghee was silent in surprise.

"This ends," Kard told her, stepping between her and the rebels. "No more slaves. No more youths sent to die for nothing."

"Impossible. No Spehari would join this scum," she snarled. "Your tricks will not—"

"I am the Right Hand of Sunset." The words were quiet, barely above a whisper. Teer wasn't sure that even Mona was meant to hear them, but *he* did.

"I am Spehari, sworn to guard the Unity and protect those who take into our charge," Kard said loudly, projecting his voice so everyone could hear him. "*This*"—he gestured to the dragon—"is not protection. You swore the same oath once, Mona of House Ghee.

"You have broken that oath. And by Pillars of Iron and Tablets of Stone, by Oaths of Will and Gifts of Magic, I condemn you for it."

Power hammered through the value as Mona wordlessly rejected him. This wasn't the fire and lightning she'd hurled at Teer. This was a blaze of pure magical energy, blue sparks forming up around her as she sent it directly at Kard.

Kard met it in kind, a tidal wave of orange sparks to Teer's sight. The power of the two Spehari *filled* the space around them, sucking even air out of the tiny ravine as they engaged in the magical equivalent of a pushing match.

It was subtler than that, Teer knew. He could see some of the currents and shifts, the feints and strikes flowing through the patterns of magic, but he wasn't sure how much anyone else saw—even the two Mages at the heart of the fight.

He'd seen his friend go all-out once. He knew that Kard was more powerful than the only other El-Spehari Teer had ever met, the Captain-Magistrate Taran. He'd known that Kard had served at the direct command of the Prince of Sunset, as a brigade commander in the Sunset Rebellion, and had to be one of the stronger El-Spehari.

He'd never realized that it was even *possible* for Kard to be stronger than a full-blooded Spehari, but he could see as his friend's power drove Mona's back. Every feint she pulled, he countered. Every trick she tried to muster, he'd clearly seen before—and the reverse wasn't true.

And Mona could tell as easily as Teer could. There was a clear moment where she realized she couldn't win the magical duel she'd started—and then she dove for the ground, releasing her side of the duel and letting Kard's power blaze down the ravine as she slid under the dragon tail.

Her hunter was in her hand and still loaded, aiming for Kard while his energy was still off-balance.

Teer still wasn't sure he could stand, but he could draw a quick-shooter and fire. Two of his shots hit the dragon-tail wagon, but at least two hit Mona—as did at least two *other* shots from Song's rebels.

She never pulled the trigger on the hunter. The gun fell from grip-less fingers as she glared silently up at Kard for a long, long moment.

———

TEER FORCED himself to his feet, walking slowly forward. Kard was breathing heavily but gave him a firm nod.

"Wagon forty-six," his friend muttered. "Maybe a dozen."

"Got it."

Teer hooked his foot under a repeater—not his, the one belonging to the grizzled sergeant he'd shot earlier, he thought—and kicked it into the air and his hands. Wagon forty-six was near the end of the dragon tail, easily a hundred feet away still.

The last of the guards had retreated during the duel between the Mages, but they were still in the fight. Or, at least, armed and upright.

He walked over the bodies of the rest of the platoon Mona had mustered to drive back the attack. Between the snipers, Teer and Kard, there were no survivors there.

He could hear the breathing of the conscripts in the wagons he walked past. Their terror sent a chill down his spine, hardening his anger. He slowly thumbed rounds into the loading gate of the repeater and stepped into the view of the windows with a fully loaded gun.

Only the two moons lit the cut now. He could see clearly into the wagon, but he suspected all the soldiers could see was a silhouette.

To discourage any clever ideas, he leapt from halfway along wagon forty-five. He caught the edge of the dragon-wagon in one hand, readjusting his jump to land perfectly on the forward entry balcony of the wagon full of armed soldiers.

The repeater pointed through the open door. There were a dozen identical weapons in the vehicle, but none of them were pointed at him.

"This is over," he told them flatly. "Drop. Your. Guns."

There was a silence that probably only *felt* like eternity, and then the first soldier obeyed. Her repeater hit the ground with a metallic clatter, and even Teer winced at the thought that it might go off by accident.

Thankfully, it was either empty or better maintained than that. The others laid their weapons down more carefully, rising back up with their hands clearly visible to him.

It was, after all, over.

25

"The prisoners are a problem."

Song's tone was flat, without any hint that she was talking about living, breathing people. Teer simply glared at her.

Firstmoon had set and thirdmoon had risen. There were still two moons in the sky, though thirdmoon was dimmer this time of season.

"Because six hundred rescuees aren't," Kard pointed out. "Do you have a plan for them?"

Teer had to hope she did, because when he and Kard had been breaking the conscripts out on their own, all they'd been able to do for them was make sure there were no records.

"That's why most of my posse were locals," Song said calmly. "They're taking people in hand; they'll help them get home. I'll get a feel for as many of them as I can along the way, see if any of them are recruitable."

"Do the same with the soldiers," Teer suggested. "Do you really think they can go back to the Unity now?"

He gestured around them. The prisoners were gathered in a group off to one side, under the guns of a trio of hard-eyed women that he suspected *weren't* locals. In the other direction, the dragon was being emptied of the last useful supplies, and a masked man Teer didn't recognize was moving along the tail, taking parcels from a pack and linking them with thin cord.

He could recognize a fuse.

"A Magistrate is dead," he continued. "A dragon has been ambushed and most of a company of the Unity Army wiped out. Those who survive aren't goin' to be rewarded for it. They're goin' to get hung over a fuckin' wardstone, Song. I know it. You know it. *They* know it."

She chuckled. There was a touch of actual amusement to it.

"And you didn't think that through when you shot to disarm, did you?" she asked. "What happens if I order my hands to finish off the witnesses?"

"Killin' the people we came to rescue would feel wrong, even to you," he countered. "And they're as much danger as the soldiers."

"And I'd have to go through you."

"And you'd have to go through *us*," Kard told her. He didn't move to loom over her or to step between her and Teer. He didn't need to. With his illusion down, only the bandana wrapped around his face concealed his identity—and it concealed neither his pale skin nor his long ears.

"A rogue Magistrate and *whatever* in Mounting Courts you are, Hunter Teer," Song conceded. "I see no reason to add to the dead today. We'll put Mona and the Unity bodies in the dragon tail. The fires and bombs will see to them. That will cover any survivors. If they're smart, they'll know they must disappear."

"If they're stupid, let's make *sure* they know," Kard suggested. "I can speak to them. I know how Unity soldiers are trained to think."

"You would." Song eyed him. "I appreciate your assistance, though I have many questions about how you came to be here, 'Hunter' Sedor."

Teer hadn't been there when Kard gave the woman a false name, but he had managed to avoid using the other man's name until he'd heard what Song called him.

"You will get no answers," Kard told her. "You need no answers.

Our common cause today saved you. And speaking of that, Mona's records?"

"I have them."

Agus appeared out of the shadows, a trio of heavy leatherbound books held in his hands. The big forester was moving slowly, a bandage wrapped around his hip where Mona's long-range shot had only barely missed gutting him.

Teer wasn't sure the man should have been walking, especially without seeing a doctor, but Agus didn't seem inclined to *stop*.

"Give them to me," Kard instructed. Agus didn't even look at Song, and Teer could tell she was annoyed by that.

That softened when Kard immediately handed her and Teer one of the books each. Teer flipped open the one in his hands and grimaced.

It was about what he'd expected. Each page was filled with neat writing in several hands, filling out carefully spaced ledgers with the names and addresses of recruits—and notes about their families.

As Kard had warned, the books would be more than enough to track down the missing recruits.

"There will be a copy in Shiaray as well," Kard murmured. "Do you have a plan for those? We do."

"I do," Song admitted. "But while it should work, it has the potential to get messy. For all that they couldn't stop this, Shiaray's Wardkeeper and Wardwatches are honest. About as good as Unity police can get, and if the plan goes wrong, at least a few of them will die."

"Then let's try ours," Teer interjected, looking over at Kard. "I don't see an issue, do you, Sedor?"

"None," Kard agreed. "And as for these... you may want to put them down."

Teer joined his friend in tossing the record book onto the ground. It took Song a moment longer to realize what he meant, and then all three books were in a rough pile on the ground.

A pile that was surrounded with orange sparks for a heartbeat and then burst into cheerful flames. Leather and paper alike rapidly started to disintegrate.

"You." Kard pointed at Agus. "Come here for a moment."

The forester obeyed. Kard placed his hand on the other man's hip, closed his eyes, and then winced.

"How are you *walking*?" he growled. "The bullet is still *in* there and your femur is cracked from one side to the other."

"Hurts a bit, but others needed the doctor more," Agus said firmly, but he was wincing at Kard's touch.

Teer saw the splash of orange power. The bandage came off in Kard's hand, and he held it up with the bullet in it.

"Get a new bandage," the mage ordered. "The bullet is out and the fractures are fixed, but you're still going to bleed. You *will*, however, still be able to walk in a few days. As you were going, you might have never walked again after tomorrow."

Agus winced, glanced over at Song, then returned to Kard.

"There are others worse hurt," he repeated. "Can ye… Can ye help them? There's a few real bad ones. One the doc said only lived 'cause someone did first aid on the spot."

"I can. Show me," Kard instructed.

That left Teer and Song alone, looking out over the cut where they'd inflicted one of the worst defeats the Unity had seen outside of the Sunset Rebellion and the Kott War.

"We can't save everyone," Teer murmured. "But we could save this lot."

"Now that we have, I can admit that I wasn't certain we could," Song told him, her voice as quiet as his. "I don't know who you and Sedor actually are, Hunter, but I know that my plans for dealing with the Magistrate clearly weren't enough.

"This was the first time I've ever gone up against one."

"Mona was the first I'd ever seen closer than riding through town from a distance," Teer admitted. "Other than Sedor, obviously. But he conceals himself and his power for his own safety."

"There aren't many Spehari who challenge the Unity," she said. "I'd love to know how you two ended up riding together."

"As he said, you need no answers," Teer replied. "We fought together tonight, but we have our own secrets."

"Like what you are, as well as what he is. I've never seen anyone fight like that before."

"We all have secrets," he repeated. He'd take a chance to walk through the rescues as they made their way back to Shiaray—hopefully scattering as they went—and see if he could identify any potential Adept trainees.

He couldn't train them yet. He needed a safe place to take them first, but he needed to be sure he *could* identify the potential.

The only other Merik he was certain had possessed Adept gifts had been Boulder... the bandit chief he'd killed to save Kard's life on their first bounty. Hopefully, he could find some candidates that *weren't* monsters.

"Secrets," Song echoed, then snorted. "I'm the left hand, Hunter. The one who doesn't tell anyone who they are or what they do.

"I know all about secrets."

26

Teer thought it was strange to be sitting in a hotel bar barely half a day's ride from the ravine where he'd just engaged in a violent act of open rebellion against the government that had ruled his people for centuries.

But no one had seen his face who would survive reporting in. Even if one of the soldiers decided that they trusted the Spehari more than was wise, it would be days yet before they could report in—and their descriptions of faces seen at a distance in the dark would be unreliable at best.

He nursed a cup of dark-brewed tea, waiting for Kard to return from the final part of the mission they'd taken on. The mage would be wearing his own face for this, since the Wardkeeper would have tools to pierce illusions, but the odds that Shiaray's Wardkeeper could identify Kard's true face were low indeed.

Teer still stretched his senses, listening for any sign of conflict or surprise elsewhere in the town and paying attention to the weak feelings he was receiving through his bond with the El-Spehari. He was utterly unsurprised to realize that Song had just stepped through the door of the bar, accompanied by the cold-eyed woman who'd been with the snipers.

He'd never caught the other woman's name, but she gave him a flirtatious smile and crossed the room to join him. The smile didn't reach her eyes, and Teer knew it was a performance for anyone else in the bar.

"Never did catch your name," he said with a false smile of his own. She was twice his age, though if he looked past her cold dead eyes, she was attractive in a sharp-edged way.

"Ilse," she told him, with a quick certainty that told him it was a lie.

That was fine. Teer had realized too late in this mess that he should be more careful with his own name. To keep himself and Kard safe, he might well have to become like his friend and choose a new name.

"Good to see you," Song said, dropping in next to Ilse. "Any problems with that business you and your friend were handling?"

"It's in hand," he told her. "Should hear soon enough. Yours?"

"Everything is moving where it should be, even the unexpected extras you gave us," she replied. "There will always be some issues with that type of cargo, but I've got some experts in to handle it."

He nodded. Rescues and prisoners alike were being moved to safety, with some of Song's outsiders—like Ilse—guiding events rather than leaving people to their own devices.

Teer had only managed to visit with a dozen or so of the rescued conscripts, but they'd all been *delighted* not to be dragged off to war in chains. He suspected many, if not most, might have been far more resigned to the draft, had it been a less-violent thing.

He wasn't sure how large a portion of the posse she'd ridden out with were fellows of Song's versus the local recruits, and he knew better than to ask. Song wasn't working alone, but he didn't expect her to tell him more than that.

"We're here to see the last business done," Song continued. "And so Ilse can make eyes at you, of course."

Teer would never pretend he was experienced with women. His experiences to date had been exclusively forward women who had decided he was easy on the eyes and would be fun in bed. The closest thing to an exception had been Lora, the Merik townswoman they'd taken out to the Kota, and they'd known from the moment they became lovers that it was a strictly limited thing. She'd had to stay among the Kota and he'd needed to leave.

Even with *his* limited experience, he could tell that the eyes Ilse was making at him were intended for the others in the bar. She was probably enjoying the view—his jacket was on the chair, and he suspected the seasons of travel and training had left him testing the limits of his better shirts.

"He's here," Teer said, gratefully latching on to his bond telling him that Kard had reached the entrance to the hotel. There hadn't been a hint of a problem at any point.

Kard walked into the hotel and Teer focused to be able to see the illusion he wore. He had put on his "Teer's cousin" face and brought up the illusion of a Hunter's duster over the burgundy Magistrate's uniform he was wearing.

Teer hadn't seen that uniform when he was going through Kard's things, but it had fit far too well to be something Kard had improvised in the two candlemarks since reaching town. It had to be Kard's—or, perhaps, *Karn's*, though Teer didn't think the Lord Colonel had dressed as a standard Magistrate.

He was carrying a traveler's knapsack and dropped that on the table in front of Song.

"You know what those are," he murmured. "It's done."

He looked over at Teer who met his gaze and nodded appreciatively. He knew how much of a risk Kard took every time he interacted with Unity bureaucracy as a Spehari.

"We will deal with them," Song promised, reaching out for the bag. "You have my word."

"A word without even a real name," Kard replied, his tone soft enough that no one away from their table could hear it—though Teer saw the orange sparks of magic that wrapped around them to keep their conversation private. Sparks that flew without, he noted, disrupting Kard's illusion.

That was different, and he wasn't sure what it meant.

"It's all I can give you, *Sedor*," she countered, and he smiled.

"I'm not denying the value of your word, Song. I just find myself concerned about tying our fate to an agitator known to the Unity. I know nothing about you."

"That is the nature of people like me," she replied. "We are the left hand of a mission that cannot fail."

Again with *the left hand…* and Teer remembered what Kard had said when he was facing Mona. No one else had heard it. Teer guessed that Kard had been speaking to himself, a reminder of another time.

The Right Hand of Sunset.

"A mission, Song?" Kard asked, but Teer sensed through the bond that he had *also* picked up the left-hand-versus-right-hand dynamic. "That's quite vague."

"Not *a* mission, Sedor. *The* mission," she corrected herself. "You know the one."

"No one else can hear us, Song. You may as well be clear instead of annoyingly vague."

Teer was probably the only one who picked up the touch of a sharp Spehari-educated accent in Kard's voice as he challenged the woman.

"The liberation of the oppressed and the destruction of the Unity," she told him, raising her chin. "Am I to believe you don't know it?"

"You know enough of what I am to be very dangerous to me," Kard said. "I do not recommend games."

Teer didn't like where this was going. He doubted Kard's magic could cover the two of them shooting their way out—and all he had on him was a single quickshooter. He'd need to get up to their room to get the rest of his gear.

"Then be clear on what you want, Sedor," Song replied. "You know who I am, from the bounties and the stories. All I know about you is that you are Spehari and fighting the Unity.

"That's enough for me. I'd recruit you in a blink if I thought you were interested, but I feel that you and your friend have another task in mind. We are allies, I think, but you walk another path."

"We do." Teer spoke without waiting for Kard, but he could sense what the other man wanted. "But I have to ask: recruit for what?"

"The mission," she repeated. She glanced around them, and Teer realized that she seemed to have been aware of Kard's sound-muffling spell before he pointed it out. She wasn't, so far as he could tell, Adept-gifted… which raised some interesting questions.

"*Whose* mission?" Kard growled. "An organization? An individual? If I would ever work with your people again, I'd like to know it."

"I think you know, Sedor," Song told him. "That's why you're asking. But either way, a rogue Magistrate is someone who should know the stakes."

She smiled, rising and taking the rucksack of records off the table. As Ilse rose with her, Song leaned over to whisper in Kard's ear—as if she was trying to keep Teer from hearing.

"I work for the Prince in Sunset."

———

Teer and Kard will return…

Never miss when new books are released by joining the mailing list at GLYNNSTEWART.COM/MAILING-LIST/

JOIN THE MAILING LIST

Love Glynn Stewart's books? Join the mailing list at:

GlynnStewart.com/mailing-list

Be the first to find out when new books are released!

ABOUT THE AUTHOR

GLYNN STEWART is the author of Starship's Mage, a bestselling science fiction and fantasy series where faster-than-light travel is possible–but only because of magic. His other works include science fiction series Duchy of Terra, Castle Federation and Vigilante, as well as the urban fantasy series ONSET and Changeling Blood.

Writing managed to liberate Glynn from a bleak future as an accountant. With his personality and hope for a high-tech future intact, he lives in Canada with his partner, their cats, and an unstoppable writing habit.

CREDITS

The following people were involved in making this book:
Copyeditor: Richard Shealy
Proofreader: M Parker Editing
Cover Artist: Elias Stern
Faolan's Pen Publishing:
Jack Giesen

And a sincere thank you to Glynn's Patreon subscribers!

OTHER BOOKS
BY GLYNN STEWART

For release announcements join the mailing
list or visit **GlynnStewart.com**

STARSHIP'S MAGE
Starship's Mage
Hand of Mars
Voice of Mars
Alien Arcana
Judgment of Mars
UnArcana Stars
Sword of Mars
Mountain of Mars
The Service of Mars
A Darker Magic
Mage-Commander
Beyond the Eyes of Mars
Nemesis of Mars
Chimera's Star
Ambassador for Mars
Chimera's Fall
The Lies Arcana
Shadow of Mars(*Upcoming)*

Starship's Mage: Red Falcon
Interstellar Mage
Mage-Provocateur
Agents of Mars

Starship's Mage Novellas
Pulsar Race
Mage-Queen's Thief

DUCHY OF TERRA

The Terran Privateer
Duchess of Terra
Terra and Imperium
Darkness Beyond
Shield of Terra
Imperium Defiant
Relics of Eternity
Shadows of the Fall
Eyes of Tomorrow

SCATTERED STARS

Scattered Stars: Conviction

Conviction
Deception
Equilibrium
Fortitude
Huntress
Prodigal

Scattered Stars: Evasion

Evasion
Discretion
Absolution

PEACEKEEPERS OF SOL

Raven's Peace
The Peacekeeper Initiative
Raven's Course
Drifter's Folly
Remnant Faction
Raven's Flag
Wartorn Stars
Raven's Hope

Prequel Novella
Honor & Renown: A Peacekeepers of Sol Novella

HOUSE ADAMANT
The Exodus Gambit
The Old Guard
The Valkyrie Strategem
Regent's Mate (Upcoming)

EXILE
Exile
Refuge
Crusade
Ashen Stars: An Exile Novella

CASTLE FEDERATION
Space Carrier Avalon
Stellar Fox
Battle Group Avalon
Q-Ship Chameleon
Rimward Stars
Operation Medusa
A Question of Faith: A Castle Federation
Novella

Dakotan Confederacy
Admiral's Oath
To Stand Defiant
Unbroken Faith

VIGILANTE
(WITH TERRY MIXON))
Heart of Vengeance
Oath of Vengeance

**Bound By Stars: A Vigilante Series
(With Terry Mixon)**
Bound By Law
Bound by Honor
Bound by Blood

AETHER SPHERES

Nine Sailed Star
Void Spheres
Fated Skies (*upcoming*)

TEER AND KARD

Wardtown
Blood Ward
Blood Adept
Adept's Path (*upcoming*)

CHANGELING BLOOD

Changeling's Fealty
Hunter's Oath
Noble's Honor
Fae, Flames & Fedoras: A Changeling Blood Novella

ONSET

ONSET: To Serve and Protect
ONSET: My Enemy's Enemy
ONSET: Blood of the Innocent
ONSET: Stay of Execution
Murder by Magic: An ONSET Novella

STANDALONE NOVELS & NOVELLAS

City in the Sky
Excalibur Lost: A Space Opera Novella
Balefire: A Dark Fantasy Novella
Icebreaker: A Fantasy Naval Thriller
Seekers in the Void: A Space Adventure